Nova rushed up the stairs with River following close behind.

They proceeded cautiously through the house, their senses heightened by the ominous atmosphere that clung to the air. A faint whimper reached their ears as they moved down a corridor lined with closed doors. The haunting sound led them to a partially open door at the end of the hallway.

With a shared nod, they approached the door, the creaking floorboards beneath their feet betraying their presence. The once-serene space was now a tableau of horror.

Nova and River entered the room, their guns drawn as they cautiously scanned the area. Their eyes fell upon the lifeless body slumped in the corner. Blood pooled around her, staining the once-white carpet a dark red.

Nova rushed to the victim's side without hesitation, checking for a pulse she knew wasn't there. Her heart sank as she realized they were too late.

Turning to River, she could see the same anger and determination she felt in his eyes.

They would not rest until they found those responsible.

SAFE HOUSE SECURITY

JACQUELIN THOMAS

INTRIGUE

Harlequin®
INTRIGUE™

Recycling programs for this product may not exist in your area.

ISBN-13: 978-1-335-45700-4

Safe House Security

Copyright © 2024 by Jacquelin Thomas

This is a work of fiction. Names, characters, places and incidents are either the product of the author's imagination or are used fictitiously. Any resemblance to actual persons, living or dead, businesses, companies, events or locales is entirely coincidental.

For questions and comments about the quality of this book, please contact us at CustomerService@Harlequin.com.

TM and ® are trademarks of Harlequin Enterprises ULC.

Harlequin Enterprises ULC
22 Adelaide St. West, 41st Floor
Toronto, Ontario M5H 4E3, Canada
www.Harlequin.com

Printed in Lithuania

MIX
Paper | Supporting responsible forestry
FSC® C021394

Jacquelin Thomas is an award-winning, bestselling author with more than fifty-five books in print. When not writing, she is busy catching up on her reading, attending sporting events and spoiling her grandchildren. Jacquelin and her family live in North Carolina.

Books by Jacquelin Thomas

Harlequin Intrigue

Guardian Defender
Safe House Security

Love Inspired Suspense

Sorority Cold Case

Love Inspired Cold Case

Evidence Uncovered
Cold Case Deceit

Love Inspired The Protectors

Vigilante Justice

Harlequin Heartwarming

A Family for the Firefighter
Her Hometown Hero
Her Marine Hero
His Partnership Proposal
Twins for the Holidays

Visit the Author Profile page at Harlequin.com.

CAST OF CHARACTERS

Nova Bennett—A dedicated US marshal assigned to the witness protection division. She holds the Mancuso cartel accountable for her father's tragic demise and wants to make them pay.

River Randolph—DEA agent on a relentless quest for justice, driven by the mission to avenge two fallen comrades as he endeavors to dismantle the formidable Mancuso cartel.

Arya de Leon—Seeks to escape from the tangled web of consequences ignited by Mateo, which now threatens to engulf her.

Mateo de Leon—Defies the WITSEC program, opting for one last daring negotiation with the Mancuso cartel—an attempt that unfolds in deadly results.

Ramona Lazano—Arya's mother.

Pablo Lazano—Arya's father.

Johnny Boyd "Johnny Boy" Raymond—Top lieutenant within the formidable Mancuso cartel, whose guiding principle is that "dead witnesses can't talk."

Kenny Latham—River's partner.

Poppy Mancuso—The head of the Mancuso cartel.

Chapter One

Deputy Marshal Nova Bennett stepped out of the elevator and walked quickly to her boss's office. She'd received an urgent call from her supervisor, Roy Cohen, almost as soon as she'd arrived at work this morning. Nova didn't know what this was about, but whenever they discussed sensitive information, they did so within the confines of his office.

She took a deep breath before knocking and letting herself in.

"Juan DeSoto was found in the trunk of his car. Shot in the head," Roy said as soon as she stepped inside.

Filled with disappointment, Nova sighed and dropped into the nearest chair. With that news, what had started as a good day in the Witness Security Division of the US Marshals Service had taken a sudden turn. According to police reports, Juan had left his office five days ago and never returned home. Nova had been hoping for a better outcome for the missing brother of her latest witness, Mateo de Leon.

Mateo, whose real name was Manuel DeSoto, was close to his brother. He'd owned an accounting firm with offices in Los Angeles and Mexico, a perfect cover for laundering money. He was a prominent, trusted member of the Mancuso cartel, overseeing many of their financial transactions—until they discovered he was stealing from them. Poppy

Mancuso, the head of the cartel, had ordered his death, and Mateo had since joined WITSEC. Nova had been his handler for the past eight months.

She tapped the oblong-shaped table before her, her nails beating a staccato rhythm with increasing intensity. Her eyes bored into Roy's as she said, "Mateo has been nothing but a thorn in our side since he entered WITSEC. Demanding a six-figure stipend, a mansion in an exclusive neighborhood, and all the country-club privileges. But now, with Juan's death, he might go over the edge. He was already angry with his brother for refusing to join him in the program."

Despite Mateo's constant complaining, she was his handler. And she'd wanted this case because of the connection to the Mancuso cartel. She wanted to help bring down the organization to avenge her father's murder. Her dad's killer, a lower-level hit man, had been arrested but died before he could stand trial. Nova would not be satisfied until Poppy Mancuso was arrested and imprisoned.

Her cell phone rang.

Recognizing the number, Nova said, "It's Mateo. I'd better take this…" She braced herself for what was to come.

As soon as she answered, the man on the other end yelled, "Johnny Boy had my brother killed! Juan didn't have nothing to do with this. The cartel…they just went and murdered him. As far as I'm concerned, it's an eye for an eye… I'm going to find Johnny Boy myself and make sure he pays for this."

John Boyd Raymond, also known as Johnny Boy, was Poppy's right hand. Before Mateo joined WITSEC, he'd placed a call to the DEA. He'd agreed to testify against Poppy and a few other prominent cartel members—including her top lieutenant—in exchange for protection for him and his wife. No doubt Johnny Boy was behind this murder, trying to lure Mateo out of hiding.

Nova heard sobbing in the background and spoke calmly. "Mateo, you can't do something reckless. I'm so sorry for your loss, but there's nothing you can do to help Juan now. You did everything you could to convince him to come to WITSEC, and he refused. Go comfort Arya. Your wife needs you."

"You expect for me just to let this go?" he demanded. "Juan was innocent. His murder must be avenged…" Mateo lapsed into Spanish as he continued to vent. "I gave up millions for this…"

Nova kept a gentle demeanor as she listened to Mateo's rant about seeking revenge for his brother's murder and how he'd given up everything to join witness protection. The news of Juan's death saddened her. She understood his grief and his desire for revenge.

"Arya's afraid for her parents, Nova," Mateo said. "And I don't know what to tell her. It's my fault that she's in this situation, but it's not like I can do anything about it. Johnny Boy and Poppy aren't gonna rest until they see me dead for betraying the cartel. I never shoulda gone to the DEA. I shoulda just kept my mouth shut and disappeared."

"You went to the DEA for help because you embezzled money from the cartel. They found out and were going to kill you," Nova stated, reminding him that it wasn't some selfless act on his part. "You wanted protection. You still *need* that protection, Mateo."

"I know that," he muttered, his tone filled with resignation.

Arya must have taken the phone from Mateo, because Nova heard her voice next.

"My parents need to be in witness protection." Her voice

faltered a moment. "That horrible Johnny Boy is going after Mateo's family. He'll kill my family next. My husband's told the DEA everything he knows about the cartel. Why hasn't the FBI or DEA—whoever—why haven't they arrested Johnny Boy and locked him up already? You all know that he's a murderer. I'm not understanding why he's still walking around free. Why are we living like...like this...? We're the ones in *prison*."

Nova clenched her jaw, trying to contain the small wave of frustration. Mateo was overcome with grief at the moment, but he couldn't forget his situation, she thought to herself, taking a deep breath to calm her nerves.

"You call this living?" Arya asked. "We gave up everything, while Johnny Boy is free to do whatever he pleases."

Johnny Boy had been a close friend of Poppy's for years. After her husband Raul's death, Poppy had taken over the Mancuso cartel, which was one of the largest importers of drugs smuggled into the United States through elaborate land and air distribution channels. She had handpicked Johnny Boy to control a large part of the cartel operations after her former lieutenant, Calderon, was arrested two years ago. Tall and dark-skinned with long dreadlocks, Johnny Boy was an unassuming man. However, his unremarkable appearance was deceptive. He was a skilled marksman with an uncanny ability to elude capture for the past ten years. He needed to be stopped.

"Arya, would you put Mateo back on the phone, please?" Nova asked.

After a pause, Mateo's voice came on the line. "Juan's death is on me, and there's nothing you can say to change that, Nova. It's up to *me* to make sure Johnny Boy and Poppy Mancuso pay for having him killed."

She listened with rising dismay before saying, "Mateo, I

can't keep you in WITSEC if you want to leave, but understand that we can't protect you if you abandon the program." Frankly, they couldn't let him walk. The DEA needed Mateo to testify in court against the cartel.

"My b-brother is dead, and I can't even attend his f-funeral." His voice broke.

"I'm sorry, Mateo."

"It bothers me that this is all my fault," he said again. "If I'd kept my mouth shut, then maybe Juan would still be alive."

"I know this isn't easy for you," she responded. She searched for something to say that might offer a small comfort to him.

"No, it's not. If it weren't for my wife, I'd go after Johnny Boy myself. But I'll let the law handle him." He released a sigh of resignation. He sounded much calmer. "I don't feel like going, but I better prepare my mind for my work shift. I'm due at my new job at three o'clock." Mateo paused momentarily, then added, "Nova, you don't have to worry. I'm not going to leave the program."

She expelled a breath. "I'm glad to hear it."

They finished their conversation and hung up.

"I'm not sure what they're mourning more—Juan or the money they had to give up," Nova said.

She stood up and walked around the table, navigating toward the door. "I'm thinking both. Mateo's a little calmer now, so I'm going to get myself a cup of tea, then try to clear some of the paperwork off my desk."

Nova stopped in the break room to make herbal tea, then walked to her work area. She sat down at her desk, eyeing the wood-framed photo of her father. A pain squeezed her heart as she thought of him. "I miss you so much," she whispered. She was thirty-three years old but still yearned for the haven her father's arms had once provided.

She placed a finger as if to stroke his grayish-blond hair. Special Agent II Easton Bennett was a man she'd always admired. He'd fallen in love with a Black woman and stood up to his parents when they voiced their disapproval. Her father didn't care. He loved her mother and had married her. It was her father's passion for his career that had inspired her to become a US marshal. He had been dedicated to his job, but it was that same dedication that ultimately led to his death at the hands of the cartel while protecting a witness.

She whispered to the face with deep-set blue eyes, "I wish I could talk to you, Daddy. I've got such a bad feeling about this... I know Mateo's going to do something stupid. Something that will get him killed." Mateo wasn't the sort of man who would let his brother's death go unanswered. She understood this particular feeling. Luis, the cartel member who'd murdered her father, died before his conviction, leaving Nova still hungering for justice.

She'd considered before that Mateo hadn't told Homeland Security and the DEA everything he knew about the cartel. A man like him, who wanted to be in control, might keep crucial information if he thought it would give him an edge. She felt terrible for his poor wife. Arya was innocent in all this. Now she was doomed to spend the rest of her life in witness protection.

Her Apple Watch notified her that it was time for movement.

Nova exited her desk and strolled outside her 9 x 9 cubby to a nearby window. She stared at the busy street down below, bustling with automobiles and people going about their business in all directions. This September weather was the perfect temperature. Not too hot or cool.

Nova had left Wisconsin two years ago in search of a place that wouldn't remind her so much of her father everywhere she went. She loved Charlotte, North Carolina, but she still missed him dearly.

Her heart filled with grief, Nova turned away from the window and returned to her desk.

She'd learned that her father's absence would follow her no matter where she went.

Nova gave herself a mental shake. She had a stack of paperwork that required her attention. Although focused on her tasks, she couldn't escape the ominous feeling swirling around in her gut.

If Mateo violated the rules of the program, then he risked having to leave WITSEC, and any criminal actions on his part could land him in prison. Nova often had to remind Mateo and Arya of the importance of this chance they'd been given.

It was an opportunity to stay alive—something the cartel would never offer them.

Los Angeles, CA

DEA SPECIAL AGENT RIVER RANDOLPH and his partner entered the federal building on East Temple Street. He and Kenny, along with a few other colleagues, had just concluded a knock-and-talk with a suspect and were returning to the office.

"I hope the rest of the day won't be as exciting as this morning," Kenny said as they strolled across the lobby.

River chuckled. "Can you believe that guy? He welcomes us into his house and then tries to run."

Earlier that morning, they'd met up with a team of ATF agents and police officers in an empty warehouse fifteen minutes away from the suspect's home.

While the team remained out of sight, River and Kenny had brazenly walked up, knocked and asked if they could search the house. Surprisingly, Rico Alfaro had given them full access, claiming he had nothing to hide.

The man had no idea he'd been under surveillance for the past twenty-four hours.

Not long after, Rico Alfaro was apprehended and brought downtown in handcuffs. River's team had found massive quantities of chemicals in the garage, just as River had suspected. They'd also found stashes of cocaine, fentanyl and amphetamines in one of the bedrooms.

River felt a sense of purpose after the bust—the weight of his fallen partner's badge hung heavy on River's chest, a constant reminder of the vow he'd made to keep illegal substances off the streets. But now, with his partner's blood staining those very streets at the hands of the ruthless cartel, it was no longer just a sense of duty that fueled River. It was pure vengeance, a burning desire to bring down every member of that cartel and make them pay for what they had taken from him.

His new partner, Kenny Latham, was an experienced DEA criminal investigator, having worked in the field for more than fifteen years since River came to the agency. At forty-two, Kenny was the type of man who faithfully went to the gym three times a week to maintain his athletic build and never touched alcohol or cigarettes. It was something they had in common. River also worked out several times a week to keep in top physical shape for his job. Both men were over six feet tall, although Kenny was a few inches shorter than River.

They walked past an open area with potted plants and chairs down a hallway to a room filled with desks grouped in clusters of four, surrounded by a wall of offices belonging to the superior agents.

River could hear the voice of a news reporter on television coming from one of the offices—the one with the open door. His attention was immediately drawn when he overheard the news of Juan DeSoto's death. River had recently inherited the file on Manuel DeSoto from his former coworker, who'd decided to leave the agency. Manuel DeSoto and his wife were in WITSEC as Mateo and Arya de Leon.

River stood at the door outside of his supervisor's office, knocked and waited for a response.

"Come in."

Special Agent in Charge Jared Rush was seated behind a large desk.

"I just heard the news about Juan DeSoto as I walked by," he said, strolling inside. He sank down in one of the visitor's chairs facing him.

"Yeah…certainly wasn't the outcome we were hoping for," Jared said. "I'd hoped we'd find the man alive."

River nodded in agreement. Mateo had handed over important evidence to the DEA—it was a shame Juan had lost his life because of it. "The cartel must be desperate to try and flesh out his brother this way."

River didn't doubt that Juan was murdered because of his brother's criminal dealings. He had reviewed several pages of notes on the man and his family. To their knowledge, Juan had been a law-abiding citizen with not so much as a speeding ticket; he'd attended church regularly and seemed devoted to his wife and children. Juan's death was meant to send a clear message to his brother. To silence him.

River's main concern now was whether Mateo would still be willing to testify against the cartel. If Mateo wavered in his decision, River's job was to convince him that testifying was still in his best interest. And if necessary, remind Mateo that he'd become a dead man when he decided to steal from Poppy Mancuso.

River would make a trip to Charlotte to see Mateo in a couple of days. Before exiting the office, he discussed a few final particulars about his trip with Jared. He was looking forward to meeting Mateo and Arya de Leon. Less so, their handler. River had stopped short when he'd learned the name of Mateo's case agent with the US Marshals.

Nova Bennett.

He shuddered inwardly at the thought that they had to interact and work another case together.

He'd read Mateo's dossier and understood the type of man he was. There wasn't much on his wife except that she denied knowing her husband's criminal deeds.

River didn't necessarily buy it as the gospel truth but decided to reserve judgment until after he met the woman. The previous agent had also noted that he believed Mateo was withholding information from the DEA. He knew more than what he'd shared with them.

Mateo had been distraught when he'd learned that he would have to turn over all the money he'd stolen to the DEA. The report said they'd recovered over three million dollars in cash hidden in his office's walls. There was nearly a hundred thousand more in two safes at his house. He'd called it his emergency fund. The man was furious when the DEA had seized his house, business and other properties.

They were a pair of high-maintenance witnesses... He wondered how Nova was faring with them. He shut that thought down. He would come face-to-face with her soon enough.

A flicker of apprehension coursed through him. It had

taken him eighteen months to erase the pain of a broken heart after she'd left.

He'd met Nova while working with her agency on a prior case nineteen months ago. When the two weeks of working together ended, River couldn't help but feel a sense of longing. They had shared countless laughs, inside jokes, and even a few blissful moments together.

He woke up one morning and was met with an empty bed and the realization that Nova had left without a word. All their memories now seemed bittersweet, knowing it was just a temporary passion fueled by late nights and adrenaline rushes until it became more profound.

River's heart ached as he remembered their stolen kisses and whispered confessions of love. River couldn't deny that what started as a fling had become genuine and meaningful. He had fallen hard and fast, and now he was left to pick up the pieces alone. But now he couldn't shake the emptiness that consumed him. As he went through the motions of his day, River couldn't help but think about Nova—the one woman he wanted desperately to forget.

He couldn't understand why Nova had disappeared without a word to him. Was it something he'd said or done? Had he imagined the connection they'd shared? Doubt crept into River's mind, clouding his memories with uncertainty. The more he dwelled on it, the more his heart sank.

His pride wouldn't allow him to chase after her. It had been easy to avoid further contact with the woman he never wanted to see again.

Until now.

THE NEXT AFTERNOON, Nova learned that another member of Mateo's family had been assassinated outside his home. She braced herself for the phone call she knew was coming.

As expected, Mateo was enraged and spouting threats.

"I'm coming out there tomorrow to see you and Arya." Perhaps she could better reassure them in person. She spent the next thirty minutes on the phone trying to calm them.

"My cousin was just murdered! Johnny Boy is gonna kill my entire family unless somebody does something to stop him. If DEA or Homeland Security don't do something, then I will."

From what Nova had learned of Johnny Boy, he was a ruthless foe and seemed fated for the drug trade. He was the son of Chilton Raymond, a drug kingpin in Jamaica, and had become involved in the family business at the age of thirteen. Johnny Boy had risen to prominence in the cartel quickly. However, he'd been forced to leave his birthplace when his father violated a pact with a Sinaloa cartel and was assassinated when Johnny Boy was eighteen years old.

Johnny Boy had come to the US to live with his uncle at age twenty. He and Poppy had connected at a party in Miami, and she'd introduced him to Raul Mancuso. Johnny Boy soon began working for the cartel, rising quickly through the ranks.

"We're taking the threats seriously, Mateo," Nova said. "However, family members not part of the program don't receive the same level of protection. Still, we're taking appropriate action to address and investigate any threats or concerns of your relatives."

"So, what does that mean?" Mateo asked. "Do they get some type of protection or not?"

"Various measures will be taken—surveillance, law enforcement intervention, and other protective measures to mitigate potential risks. I want you to know that the safety of your family members is a priority. Law enforcement will assess and respond to threats accordingly. I want you to know that their well-being is a top priority."

As she spoke those words, her mind raced with possible scenarios and plans to protect those under her care. She couldn't afford any mistakes or lapses in security, not when the lives of her witnesses were at stake. Nova was determined to do everything she could to keep everyone safe.

"As long as you stay put, he won't find you," she said. "Do not contact any of your family members, Mateo. This is what the cartel wants. They want you out of hiding."

"I hear you," he responded.

"Do you *really*?" Nova asked. She couldn't shake the dull ache of foreboding that had persisted since Juan's murder. "Don't do something stupid, Mateo." She felt like her words were falling on deaf ears.

It's gonna be a long day, Nova thought to herself after her conversation with Mateo ended.

Her phone rang for a second time, and her heart began to race as she saw the caller ID. The Los Angeles area code flooded her mind with memories of River.

"Hello," she answered cautiously.

"Nova, it's River," he said, his voice bringing back all the emotions she had tried to bury the past couple of years.

"River…hey…" she managed, her heart pounding. "What can I do for you?"

"I'm coming to Charlotte," he announced without preamble. "We need to discuss your witnesses. I'm sure you're aware that Juan DeSoto was killed. I need to speak with his brother. Make sure he's still going to testify."

"Another member of his family has been murdered. His cousin Julio. Neither he nor Juan had any cartel affiliations."

There was a pause on the line. "They're trying to get Mateo out of hiding," River responded.

"That's what I told him. I will try to get protection for his aunt and Juan's family. Have them moved to a safe house."

"Any other family members in Los Angeles?"

"No. The rest of his family is in South America," Nova stated. "When will you arrive?"

"Tomorrow."

"I'm…I'm planning to see Mateo and his wife in the morning." She hesitated, her heart racing at the thought of facing him again. Would he even want to see her? "I'll send you their address, and you can meet me there." Despite the excitement and nerves coursing through her, Nova couldn't deny that seeing him after all these years would bring up a mix of emotions—both longing and fear of the unresolved conflicts between them.

"That's all I need from you," he replied flatly.

She felt a twinge of disappointment at River's lack of emotion. Part of her wanted him to show some enthusiasm that they'd be working together again.

As the clock struck quitting time, Nova considered canceling out meeting up with her best friend, Jersey, at the Golden Pier, a popular spot in uptown Charlotte where local law enforcement went to unwind over drinks.

By the time she reached her car, Nova decided she needed to unwind. She needed to take her mind off the case for a bit.

Her friend met her at the door.

"Perfect timing," Nova said in greeting.

"Hectic day?" Jersey asked after they sat at a table near the bar area shaped like a boat.

Nodding, she responded, "It's been a trying few days, to say the least."

Nova ordered a glass of red wine, and her friend chose white.

While waiting for their drinks to arrive, she said, "I'm

so glad it's Friday." It didn't mean much that it was the weekend, because she'd be driving out to Burlington first thing in the morning to check on Mateo and Arya. But she needed the short reprieve.

"So am I," Jersey murmured as she released her long reddish locs from the hair band that held them hostage. "I'm glad I'm not on call this weekend. I've had a busy week." Her friend was a homicide detective for the Charlotte-Mecklenburg Police Department. "I wore my murder boots more than my heels."

"You're the only person I know who has murder boots," Nova said with a chuckle. "And bright yellow ones at that." Jersey always wore rain boots whenever she visited a crime scene.

"I'm not messing up a good pair of shoes while looking for evidence," Jersey responded. "I can just rinse off my boots and keep it moving."

A couple of middle-aged men sat at a table across the room. One worked with the Marshals Service, while the other was an assistant district attorney. The assistant DA made eye contact with them and gave a slight nod in greeting.

"What's up with you and Matt?" Nova asked in a low whisper as their drinks arrived. "He can't seem to take his eyes off you."

"He keeps telling me that he wants us to try again," Jersey answered, turning her face away from him to Nova.

"How do you feel about it?"

"I don't know." Jersey shrugged. "I still love him, but I'm just not sure we belong together. Sometimes it's best not to revisit the past."

Nova picked up the menu and opened it.

Jersey sipped her wine, then asked, "What about you? Have you met anyone interesting?"

"Not really."

"You're a borderline workaholic, Nova," Jersey stated.

"You're probably right," she responded with a slight shrug.

"What about that DEA agent, River?"

Nova gave a choked, desperate laugh. "What about *him*? It's been *two* years. I'm pretty sure by now he's found someone else and is incredibly happy." She tried to keep her expression bland, but she couldn't ignore the ache in her heart whenever she thought of him. She wouldn't tell Jersey just yet about the call they'd had—or the fact she'd see him tomorrow.

Jersey studied her for a moment before replying, "I can tell by the look on your face that you don't really mean that. Don't you think it's about time you and River had a conversation?"

Nova placed a hand over her face convulsively. "About *what*?"

"Well…the way y'all left things, for one."

"You just said that sometimes it's best not to revisit the past—I agree," Nova said smoothly.

"I was referring to *my* situation."

"I know that. But it can apply to my personal life as well."

Jersey's greenish-gray eyes rested on hers. "There's just one huge difference with you and River. Y'all left a lot unsaid on the table."

"I told you that things moved at an alarming pace between us, Jersey," she stated with a hint of sadness in her voice. "It was overwhelming and I couldn't keep up." She paused, her eyes clouded with memories. "We spent every waking moment together for two weeks straight. It was all-consuming and it scared me. I needed to take a step back and figure out what I really wanted."

"Maybe for you," she responded. "But how do you know that he feels the same way?"

"Jersey, I know you mean well, but what River and I had is over and done with," Nova stated. "I admit I could've handled things better with him, but I can't rewind the clock. Besides, I spoke with him earlier. He'll be in town tomorrow to discuss a case."

Jersey's eyebrows shot up in disbelief. "How was it? Talking to River after all this time?"

"It was just business," Nova responded. "He told me he was coming to Charlotte. I said okay."

Although Nova continued to put on a facade of nonchalance for her friend, she felt an acute sense of loss deep down.

She shoved that aside as they gave their food order to the server who'd come to their table.

Jersey stood up. "I'm going to talk to Matt for a few minutes. I'll be right back."

"Take your time," Nova said.

She glanced around, taking in her surroundings. The servers were dressed in nautical uniforms. Nova soaked in the laughter and the various conversations that danced upon each interval just a tad higher than the soft musical notes playing in the background. She studied the muted colors of the bottles behind the bar.

A platter of hot wings was delivered to their table.

Nova placed six on her plate but waited for Jersey to return to dive in.

"Sorry about that. I didn't mean to be gone so long," her friend said when she sat down ten minutes later.

"I was just about to get started without you."

"Well, I appreciate you." Jersey stabbed her fork into

a wing, placing it on her plate. "Oh, I ordered us another glass of wine."

"Thanks," Nova said. She dipped a lemon-pepper drumette into ranch dressing, and the conversation turned to lighter topics.

After eating, Nova left the restaurant, heading home while Jersey stayed behind with Matt.

They are so getting back together, Nova thought to herself.

She tried but couldn't remember the last time she'd been on a date. Her focus for the last year and a half had been advancing her career. However, Nova was slowly realizing she was ready for a new career challenge.

There was a time when she didn't want anything other than to walk in her father's footsteps as a US marshal, but it hadn't been the same for her since Easton's death. She still wanted to go after the Mancuso cartel but had been thinking about switching law enforcement agencies to have a more active role in the fight against drug trafficking.

Nova glanced over at the clock on her nightstand. In a few hours, she would come face-to-face with River. Her heart raced as memories flooded her mind, the weight of regret pressing against her chest. She had always been a free spirit, drifting wherever the wind took her. And two years ago, when River had hinted that he wanted a future with her, she couldn't bear the thought of being tied down. It wasn't in her nature.

So, Nova ran.

But now she found herself questioning her choices. Had running away indeed been the right decision?

She sat in the middle of her bed, contemplating what to say when she saw him.

Nova had to prepare emotionally for facing him again. She didn't have a solid explanation for why'd she done a disappearing act. She cared deeply for River, and those feelings had scared her.

If someone asked her why, Nova couldn't provide an answer.

The clock ticked relentlessly, its sound echoing through the quiet room.

Nova couldn't understand why she struggled with commitment. The lingering doubt of what could have been if she hadn't run away that fateful night consumed her thoughts. It was a question that haunted her, even though she had accepted long ago that it would never be answered.

Deep down, Nova knew that the real reason for her reluctance stemmed from losing her father. His sudden passing had left a hole in her heart and a fear of getting too close to anyone else for fear of losing them, too. This realization only added to the weight of her doubts and fears, making it all the more difficult for her to let go and open up to love.

Chapter Two

Nova got up early to make the hour-and-forty-four-minute drive to the quaint town of Burlington. She was vigilant, making sure no one was following her. Not that she expected to be followed, but one couldn't be sure. She always took extra precautions whenever she went to a witness's house.

She exited off I-85 and took Freeman Mill Road to a small neighborhood near the Friendly Center.

Ten minutes later, Nova pulled into the driveway of a modest two-story house on a corner lot with two sizable, colorful rosebushes adorning the front.

She took a deep, calming breath before walking to the porch. Mateo and his wife were going to find a way to work her nerves.

Nova admired the two giant Boston ferns in hanging baskets before ringing the doorbell. Arya had gifted hands when it came to plants and flowers.

She found the door unlocked—the lock looked like it had been tampered with, putting her on instant alert.

Nova entered the house, hand on her duty weapon.

The tiny hairs on her neck stood to attention, and her pulse raced. Her internal warning system screamed, but she couldn't abandon her charges.

After thoroughly searching the main level and finding

no one, she went upstairs, relieved she hadn't stumbled across their bodies.

Nova was about to walk into the master bedroom when she heard a sound behind her. She glimpsed a shadowed figure in her peripheral view. She prepared to defend herself when another masked intruder shoved her back into the hall. Taken by surprise, Nova managed to get her gun in hand, but before she could get a shot off, the intruder's gloved fist slammed into her face, making her eyes water.

He went for her gun and ripped it out of her hand.

Dizzy and disoriented, she used every ounce of strength to land a punch to the intruder's gut; the force of it loosened her gun from the man's grasp and sent it sliding across the floor.

Lightning flashed before her eyes as another fist hurtled into her. Nova fought off her assailant with her full might. She scratched, pummeled and kicked, then grabbed the lamp off a hall table and smashed it down on her attacker.

The second intruder hit her on the head with something, causing white-hot pain to flash through her brain before everything went black.

AS RIVER APPROACHED his destination, his heart began to race and his palms grew sweaty. He had avoided seeing Nova for the past eighteen months, but now he couldn't escape it. As he pulled into the driveway, his eyes landed on a black SUV. His thought was that it belonged to her.

Dread filled his stomach as he parked next to the vehicle. Seeing Nova again after all this time made him realize how much he had missed her, but also how much he feared her presence.

He took a deep breath and exhaled slowly before getting out to walk up the front steps.

River had barely touched the door when it swung open. Warning prickled at the back of his neck as he stepped over the threshold. He could practically hear his heart beating over the silence.

He pulled out his duty weapon, raising it at shoulder level as he cautiously entered the house.

River checked out the kitchen and dining area. Faded traces of sunlight penetrated through the large window along the opposite wall, casting shadows in the living room.

"Mateo?" he called out. "This is Special Agent River Randolph with the DEA... Deputy Marshal Bennett...?"

The sense that something was off felt even stronger now. River's eyes darted around, searching for the slightest movement. He moved deeper into the house, then walked back to the front door. He looked upward to the second-floor railing before making his way slowly up the stairs.

As he approached the landing, River saw Nova crumpled on the floor outside of a bedroom. Unconscious.

His heart leaped to his throat as he knelt to check her pulse. *Please let her be okay. She's got to be fine.* Her pulse beat faintly against his fingers. River called for paramedics and the police.

He examined Nova while waiting for the EMTs to arrive. He wanted to make sure she was still breathing. River couldn't bear the thought that she might be seriously wounded. Someone must have been here when she arrived.

After Nova was taken to the hospital, River stayed behind with the two police officers who were processing the house as a crime scene. He walked slowly through the house where Mateo and Arya had lived for the past several months, scanning his surroundings.

The living room looked fine, except for the bookcases. It

looked like someone had rummaged through them, searching for something.

When he entered the master bedroom, River found the space in disarray. Items of women's clothing were strewn across a chair in one corner. Several drawers were left open, and it looked as though someone had rifled through them. The closet door was ajar, revealing empty hangers and abandoned shoeboxes.

He walked over and peered inside to get a closer look. There was only one piece of luggage inside. Indentations in the carpet showed there were at least two suitcases missing. *Looks like someone packed in a hurry*, he thought to himself.

There were signs of forced entry when they examined the back door. Someone had broken into the house, but he didn't think they'd found what they sought. When he found no vehicle in the garage, River was pretty sure that Mateo and Arya were on the run. And he wasn't happy about it.

He went back to the bedroom for a second, more thorough observation.

The room was in disarray, with drawers and cabinets left open as if someone had frantically searched for something. River knew it wasn't just a coincidence. The intruder must have been looking for something specific, and they likely heard Nova enter the house. They knocked her out and quickly disappeared, leaving behind a trail of destruction in their wake. It was clear that they were determined to find whatever it was they were after.

An hour later, River was at the hospital checking on Nova. He stood outside her room, silently debating whether to go inside. He'd been told her injury wasn't life-threatening, which was a relief to him. Despite how he felt about her, he didn't want any harm to come to her.

He peeked inside.

Nova lay on her side, buried under a couple of blankets.

River noted that she was more beautiful than he remembered. Lying in that hospital bed, a bandage on her forehead, Nova looked much younger than her thirty-three years. When they'd first met, she wore her hair in a cute pixie cut, which had grown out, reaching well past her shoulders. The warm brown tendrils and golden highlights complemented the glow of her honey complexion. Faint freckles were speckled across her nose.

Unexpected and disquieting thoughts raced through his mind; River's heart rate increased every time he pictured Nova's smile. His mouth tightened as he remembered how she'd treated him at the end of their assignment.

After a romantic evening filled with talk of a possible future together, River woke up to find himself alone. He had left his room foolishly searching for Nova, only to discover she'd already checked out of the hotel. She didn't even bother to leave a note behind. He'd witnessed firsthand the way she handled herself in dangerous situations, so River had never thought Nova was the type of woman who would run away.

Nova moaned softly, then shifted her position slightly.

River eased back toward the door.

She had hugely gotten under his skin, and when she'd left, she'd disappeared when he needed her the most. River shook his head as if to ward off the thought. It wasn't something he wanted to admit to himself.

NOVA OPENED HER eyes and looked around. She felt dizzy and weak but alert enough to recognize that she was in a hospital. Judging from the royal blue curtain that walled off the space, which was big enough for a bed and a chair, she was in the emergency department.

It took her a moment to remember what had happened. Her memory cleared from its foggy state—someone had jumped her. Maybe two people. Nova squeezed her eyes shut, trying to remember exactly what had taken place at the de Leon home.

Bracing herself against the pain, she placed a shaky hand on her face, which still throbbed with a dull ache. Her eyes were sensitive to the lighting in the room. She closed then opened them a few times, trying to adjust her gaze. She heard someone moaning softly in the bed next to her. Not only could she hear every groan and the private conversation between the patient and family member, but she could also smell the vomit.

The sickening odor caused Nova's stomach to churn in rebellion. She swallowed the sourness that threatened to come up and silently commanded the stirring in her belly to calm down.

Nova glimpsed a couple of nurses in light blue scrubs walking past her room. Wincing, she put a hand once again to her forehead.

Out of the corner of her eye, she glimpsed a slight curtain movement.

Nova's eyes widened as she spotted River walking toward her, his close-cropped hair perfectly framing his face. His almond-colored skin seemed to glow in the sunlight, highlighting every chiseled feature. Despite the pain that spiked through her head, she couldn't help but admire how handsome he still was, just like she remembered him. "River... what are you doing here?"

"I told you I was coming to Charlotte, remember?"

"I do," she responded after a moment.

"I found you unconscious at the house."

Nova blinked. "You brought me here?"

"No. I called the paramedics," River responded. "Did you happen to see who hit you?"

"Everything happened so fast. All I know is that there were two people in the house. I had one down, and the other hit me with something. I don't know what."

"Nova…how long have you known Mateo and his wife were thinking about running?"

River's accusatory tone made Nova sit up in bed. "Mateo was upset, but I'd hoped I'd convinced him to stay in the program. There were intruders in their home. There is the possibility that they might have been kidnapped." She winced from the throbbing ache of her head.

"I don't think so," River responded.

She peered over at him. "Why do you say that?"

"Kidnappers wouldn't have taken the time to pack clothes," he replied. "Two pieces of luggage are missing and so is the vehicle. It looks like they *ran* off before the intruder arrived."

"We have to find them," Nova said as she slipped from under the covers. "I'll initiate a search for the SUV."

"You're not going anywhere," he said. "The doctor hasn't released you."

"I can't just sit here either."

"Do you have any idea where Mateo might have gone?" River asked.

"I'd say Los Angeles. He was really upset over the deaths of his brother and cousin. He wants revenge. As for Arya, she most likely went to her parents' home in San Diego. She's been really worried about them. From what I understand, she and her mother were extremely close."

Nova's gut twisted with guilt. She should have been watching them more closely. They were her witnesses, under her protection, and now they were missing. Her heart raced with worry for their safety, knowing how consumed with rage one had been and how anxious the other was about her family. It was all too much, a constant nagging that kept Nova on edge, unable to relax until she found them safe and sound.

He shook his head no. "I don't think she's with her parents. Since Juan's death, I've had someone watching them, and there's been no sighting of Arya."

Mateo and Arya's disappearance made her head pound even worse. "I hope you're wrong about this."

"I've been wrong about many things, but this isn't one of them," River stated.

Nova stiffened. She had a feeling he was referring to his past relationship with her. But she was too weak to mount up a defense, so she let the comment slide for now. She and River had more pressing matters that required their full attention.

Chapter Three

River was all business with Nova. "You know that Mateo called the DEA after an attempt was made on his life," he said.

"Yeah." She nodded. Mateo knew how far the cartel would go to get to him and yet he'd fled.

"He embezzled money from them. They won't forget that. So, why do you think he'd risk leaving the program?" River asked. "Do you really think it's about revenge for Juan's and Julio's deaths?"

"Obviously, you think it's something more," Nova responded. "What's your theory?"

"I believe it's because Mateo had something he assumed was important enough to bargain with. I agree with the agent who did the original interview. He suspected that Mateo withheld crucial information from us. If this is true, then it's possible that he's out there trying to negotiate for his and Arya's life."

"Randolph called to update me on your condition." Roy Cohen's voice made them both look toward the entrance.

The appearance of her supervisor at the hospital caught her by surprise.

Something's wrong. She could tell by the grave expression on Roy's face. His pale complexion almost matched the yellowish-blond color of his hair.

"What's happened now?" she asked. "Has another one of Mateo's relatives been murdered?"

"Not a relative," Cohen answered, closing the curtain behind him. "This time it was Mateo."

Shock coursed through her body. "*What?* When?"

Cohen shook his head. "Mateo flew to Los Angeles last night... And now he's dead."

After she found her voice, Nova said, "That's why I drove to Burlington. I wanted to assess the situation. I knew Mateo was upset over Juan's death. I wanted to make sure he didn't do anything like leave the program."

"Airport surveillance shows that he was traveling alone."

"I can't believe this..." She muttered a string of profanity under her breath. "I told Mateo to stand down..." After a moment, she asked, "Where's my phone?"

"Nova, you need to rest," River said.

"I need my phone."

He handed it to her.

She immediately called Arya's number.

No answer.

Nova tried it several times over the next half hour.

Still no answer.

She left a message saying, "Arya, this is Deputy Marshal Bennett. I need you to return my call as soon as possible." She knew Arya was the anxious type, and Mateo's death would only make her anxiety worse.

She looked over at River. "There's a chance that Arya stayed behind but she's gone into hiding somewhere. I feel in my gut that she's in trouble."

"She is in just as much danger as Mateo was," he agreed. "Arya may actually have knowledge of what her husband did for the cartel, or the cartel suspects Mateo told her everything."

Nova folded her arms and said, "She told the last DEA agent assigned to the investigation that Mateo had kept her in the dark. She thought her husband was an accountant for high-profile clients—not that he was involved in something illegal. According to her, Arya only discovered the truth when he decided to go into the program."

"Mateo gave us copies of cartel files, but I strongly feel he didn't give us everything. The last agent who touched the file felt the same way. Mateo knew where most of the bodies were buried, so he knew way more than he told us."

"You seem pretty sure about this?" Cohen interjected.

"I've known Mateo for a few years. He came up a few times in other investigations. From what I know about him, that was his character. He was stealing from the cartel, so it's not beneath him to try to blackmail Johnny Boy and Poppy. Especially if he thought he could get enough money to stay alive."

"Okay, you might be right about Mateo, but that doesn't mean he told Arya anything. Mateo told me that he kept her from his business dealings with the cartel."

"Nova, she's the only person Mateo trusted," River stated.

She slowly swung her legs to the edge of the bed and braced herself for the head rush. "I need to see the doctor. I have to get out of here." Nova pressed the call button.

"You should try and rest for a while," River said.

"I agree," Cohen commented.

"I told you both that I'm good," she responded. "We have to find Arya."

When the nurse came, Nova told her, "I need to see the doctor. I'm ready to get out of here. I'm in the middle of an investigation."

"He'll be here as soon as he's done with another patient."

"Thank you," she replied.

The doctor walked into the room.

"I'll be outside," River said.

"You don't have to leave," Nova responded. "This shouldn't take long."

The doctor conducted a series of neurological and cognitive examinations and then ordered an MRI.

"Don't leave until I get back?" she told both men. Nova suddenly didn't want to be alone. Her anxiety level was always high whenever she had to undergo any medical assessments.

"Sure," River responded, while Cohen nodded in agreement.

After the MRI, Nova was returned to her room, and River was nowhere to be found.

Disappointment washed over her that he hadn't kept his word. It was soon blocked by the memory that she'd disappeared on him. Maybe this was some form of payback.

"He stepped out to make some phone calls," Cohen said.

River hadn't left. Her body sagged with relief as she eased back into the hospital bed. She didn't want to examine that reaction too closely. River was here for work—it was nothing personal.

"CAN I COME IN?" River asked from the doorway a few minutes later.

"Yeah. C'mon in…"

The doctor swept into the room behind River. "You have a concussion… We want to keep you overnight for observation."

Nova shook her head. "No. I need to go home."

"You have to physically and mentally rest to recover from a concussion," the doctor said. "Although you have a minor concussion, if you try to return to your regular activities too early, there is a risk of another concussion. You should wait until all your symptoms are gone before resuming normal activities."

"How long can these symptoms last?"

"In many cases, symptoms of a minor concussion resolve within a few days to a couple of weeks," the doctor responded.

When he left the room, Nova eyed her supervisor and River. "Great. I'll be fine in a few days. I've always healed fast."

"Nova, you could've been killed," Cohen stated.

"I know. The good news is that I wasn't." She sighed in frustration. "I can't believe I have to stay here in this hospital."

"It's just one night," River responded.

Nova surprised him by asking, "Will you stay with me?"

He met her gaze before looking away. "I have to go back to the house and speak with the police."

River glimpsed a shadow of disappointment in her eyes before it disappeared.

"Oh. Okay," she said.

"I want to make sure I didn't miss anything earlier." He didn't know why but he felt the need to explain. "I'll come back here if it's not too late. In the meantime, you need to rest."

"What I really need is to get out of this hospital," Nova responded. "I'm so over it already."

River knew why she didn't like hospitals. They'd talked about it during the two weeks they'd spent together. He also despised this environment because it served as a constant reminder of vulnerability and mortality. Every sterile smell, clinical beep and antiseptic surface reinforced his discomfort. But pain of any kind was a sign of weakness, as far as River was concerned. In the thirty-five years he'd been in this world, he'd cried twice: when he realized his mother never wanted him, and at the death of the woman who did—his grandmother.

He knew Nova associated hospitals with her own fragility, stemming from witnessing the decline of her paternal grandmother when she was sixteen.

Turning up her nose, Nova uttered, "The smells…the white coats and scrubs…" She shuddered. "I just can't stand being in here."

"Don't give the nurses a hard time." River walked toward the curtain. "I'd better get out of here."

"Now you're the one running away," Nova muttered beneath her breath. Could she blame him? River had every right to be skittish where she was concerned. But they would have to put aside their feelings to work together.

BY THE TIME River returned to the hospital, Nova had been moved into a private room for the night. He took the elevator to the fourth floor and stood outside her door until a nurse asked, "Are you okay?"

"Yes, I'm fine," he responded. "She's resting, and I didn't want to disturb her."

"She's been expecting you."

"The other visitor…is he still here?" River inquired.

The nurse shook her head no. "He left when she was moved to this room."

River eased inside, careful not to disturb Nova.

She was asleep, almost buried under the thin bedcovers.

He'd never forgotten her mesmerizing brown eyes or the way his body reacted when she locked gazes with him. Her long lashes brushed the top of her cheeks, almost kissing the freckles sprinkled across the bridge of her nose.

Nova had come close to dying earlier. Although they

hadn't been on speaking terms, River didn't want anything bad to happen to her.

A soft moan interrupted his thoughts. Nova shifted her position but didn't wake up.

Silently, River slid into the chair meant for visitors and suppressed a shiver as the antiseptic smell of the hospital surrounded him. He hated this place, with its sterile walls and constant reminders of death. It brought back painful memories of his grandmother's final days, fighting a losing battle against cancer. And now he was here again, by Nova's side.

He couldn't let himself get too close to her. But for now, he would stay by her side until she woke up and he could leave this place once again.

While she slept, River reviewed the information he had on her witnesses. He and Nova shared a common goal. They both wanted to find Arya de Leon. Her husband had been a valuable informant for the DEA, providing them with crucial information on drug trafficking operations. However, upon further investigation, they discovered that there were significant gaps in his reports.

Files from certain years were missing, and it appeared that large sums of money could not be traced or accounted for. This raised suspicions and cast doubt on the validity of his testimony. The DEA team knew they had to tread carefully as they delved deeper into this tangled web of deceit and illegal activities. It would mean a win for the agency if River could fill in the missing pieces. Not to mention his career.

His last two investigations had resulted in significant busts. River felt he was on a winning streak and didn't want to lose focus. He wanted to prove something to himself and those who never thought he'd amount to much.

It was too bad Mary, the woman who'd given him up at birth, was gone.

He had been a very angry kid and was constantly in trouble for fighting and skipping school. And then he'd been recruited to play for an AAU basketball team when he was fourteen. The coach had watched him playing street ball and thought he showed promise.

River had flourished under the tutelage of his coach/mentor, eventually graduating with a 3.99 GPA. He'd attended college on an athletic scholarship, joining the DEA after graduation.

He and his former coach still kept in touch. The man was there for River when his grandmother passed away four years ago and again when Mary had died in March.

Nova turned from one side to the other, and River observed her for a moment, then looked away. He settled back against the cushion of the chair and closed his eyes. The events of the day were catching up with him.

NOVA SAT UP in bed, looking around. A smile tugged at her lips when she saw River across from her, sound asleep in what had to be the most uncomfortable chair.

Almost as if he'd felt her eyes on him, River woke up.

"Good morning," she said, trying to sound cheerful.

He brushed at his eyes. "G'morning. How are you feeling?"

"I still have a little bit of a headache, but other than that I feel fine." Nova gestured toward the chair he was sitting in. "How could you sleep in that?"

"It's more comfortable than it looks," River responded. "The nurse told me it converts into a cot, but I hadn't planned on falling asleep."

Nova moved to the edge of the bed and then swung her

legs outward. "I'm gonna take a shower. Hopefully, the doctor will come by soon, and I'll be able to get out of here."

She slowly made her way across the room.

In the bathroom, she stood close to the mirror, checking out the bruises on her forehead.

Nova removed the hospital gown and got into the shower.

The hot water didn't do much to soothe her aching body, but she hadn't expected otherwise. She just wanted a bath.

Two knocks reverberated through the bathroom door.

Nova turned off the water and then got out. "Yeah?"

"I was checking to make sure you're okay," River said through the door.

"I'm good."

"Okay."

Nova grabbed a towel and dried off.

She slipped on a T-shirt and a pair of leggings that were in the large handbag she had with her. Nova took a deep breath and then walked out of the bathroom.

"Do you know if my gun was recovered?" she asked.

"I have it," River responded.

Nova was relieved. "Thank you for keeping it safe."

She tried to hide her joy at being back in bed. She felt accomplished in not having to ask River for help. If they were on better terms, it was possible Nova wouldn't feel the way she did.

He hadn't been rude to her, but he was very distant. Even now, they sat in the room in a pregnant silence, waiting for the doctor to arrive.

River got up and walked over to the window, looking out.

"How long do you intend to be in town?" Nova asked.

"Until I speak with Arya."

"I'm not sure she'll be of much help to you, River. She

had nothing to do with anything," she responded, keeping her voice low.

Their conversation came to a halt when the doctor entered the room.

An hour later, Nova was released from the hospital.

"Thanks for having my car brought here," she said as River held the door open for her.

"Are you sure you can drive yourself back to Charlotte?" he asked. "You can ride with me."

"I'm good," Nova responded. "The headache is pretty much gone now. No dizziness or double vision. I'll be fine."

"I'll be following you. If you need help, just pull to the side of the road."

"Thank you, but I'm sure I'll be okay."

Nova didn't drive off right away. Her head was consumed with thoughts of Arya and her safety, trying to come up with ideas of where she could have gone. So far, nothing had come back on the license tag.

She was acutely aware that River was sitting patiently in his vehicle waiting.

When it looked as if he were about to get out of his car, Nova started the car and left the hospital parking lot.

He followed her to I-40.

Three and a half miles later, they took the exit to I-85 South. Nova noticed that River stayed at least two cars behind her. It was as if he was sending the message that he intended to keep her at arm's length.

Nova felt the stirrings of guilt and regret over how she had walked out of River's life without so much as a word to him. At the time, she didn't know what to say to the man she'd fallen in love with but hardly knew. She'd panicked, and the only thing she could think to do was run away.

Nova assumed he must have had regrets, too, because

she'd never heard from River afterward. His lack of communication validated her belief that she'd made the right decision. Still, she was bothered by the remoteness she'd glimpsed in his gaze earlier.

Could he forget what we shared so easily?

Swallowing her apprehension, Nova chewed on her bottom lip as she drove. As much as she wanted to forget, she couldn't. The first time she and River had made love was forever etched in her mind. It was when Nova realized she'd fallen in love with him. That realization had shaken her to the very core.

The intensity of her feelings for River scared her, forcing Nova to flee despite knowing she couldn't move on with someone else. The truth was that he wasn't a man who could be easily replaced.

Now he could barely look at or stand around her. Not that Nova could blame him, given how she'd left things between them.

I should have written River a note or something. He deserved better from me.

She couldn't undo what had transpired between them. Nova considered it a waste of time to dwell on something she could not change.

She wondered if he'd met a woman who loved him freely and without reservation. The thought didn't sit well with her, but she couldn't blame River. After all, she was the one who'd chosen to walk away.

An hour and forty-five minutes later, Nova walked into her town house. She'd half expected River to follow her all the way home or at least call to see if she was okay.

Silence. He didn't call or come by.

He's really over me.

Nova choked down her disappointment. Forcing River

from her mind, she navigated to her home office. Seated at her desk, Nova placed a quick call to check in with her supervisor. She pulled out a bottle of Tylenol from the side drawer and tossed one in her mouth, followed by sips of room-temperature bottled water.

Nova settled back in her chair, waiting a few minutes for the pain to subside.

A photograph fell out when she picked up the folder lying on her desk.

It was of Mateo and his wife.

Nova admired the locket Arya always wore around her neck. It was a lovely piece of jewelry. Her mother had one that was given to her by her grandmother, but she hardly ever wore it.

Nova pushed away from her desk and stood up.

She walked over to a painting and removed it to reveal a built-in safe. She opened it and tossed the file inside. She kept all the physical files on her witnesses locked up for security. The copies on her computer were all encrypted as well.

She thought back to what River had said about Arya. Nova had to find her before the cartel did.

Chapter Four

There had always been an undeniable magnetism between River and Nova, which probably explained why he was sitting in his rental car down the street from her town house. River wanted to make sure she'd arrived home safely. But he didn't want her to know that he cared this much about her well-being.

He hated seeing her again. It had taken him two years to get her out of his system. River certainly didn't want to work with her, but he had no choice. She was Arya's handler, and he needed her assistance finding the woman. He didn't doubt that Nova would do whatever she could to keep Arya safe and in WITSEC.

After an hour passed, River felt she'd pretty much settled in for the rest of the day, so he headed to his hotel. He had only planned to be in town long enough to talk to Mateo, but now that he was dead and his wife missing…River's stay would be extended. He knew Nova had initiated a trace on the vehicle owned by Mateo and Arya. In the meantime, he decided to comb the file once more.

He spent the afternoon watching hours of video taken during Mateo's interrogation. Outside of handling finances and laundering money for the cartel, Mateo had also assisted in securing stash houses where thousands of kilograms of cocaine were unloaded from tanker trucks and then reloaded with weapons and money headed to and from California, Mexico and Arizona. During his involvement with the Mancuso cartel, he had extensive knowledge of shipments of cocaine, fentanyl and other drugs worth several billions of dollars.

Mateo had been a valuable asset for the DEA; the wealth of information and evidence he had against John Boyd Raymond made him a coveted witness. The notorious criminal sat atop the FBI's Ten Most Wanted Fugitives list, hunted by every law enforcement agency in the country. But for the DEA, it was personal. They were determined to bring Johnny Boy to justice for the cold-blooded murder of two of their agents. For River, one of the fallen agents had been like a brother, fueling his burning desire for vengeance and driving him to do whatever it took to see Johnny Boy behind bars.

River ordered room service and then made a phone call to his partner.

"Hey, Kenny. Thanks for the information on Pablo and Ramona Lozano." He'd had his partner help with the surveillance of Arya's parents, and so far, there had been little movement from the couple. "Do me a favor and keep them under surveillance for a few more days. Their daughter may show up there. Let me know as soon as she does."

"How is Nova doing?"

"She's fine," River responded. He'd called Kenny to update him after Nova was taken to the hospital. "No real damage done. She's at home now."

"Did you two get a chance to talk things over?"

"About the witness…yes, we did."

"You know that's not what I was talking about," Kenny

responded. "You and Nova need to have a conversation about what happened."

"I told you that what Nova and I had is long over. I'm not about to rehash the past. The only thing between us now is our dead witness's missing wife."

"If you say so..."

"I do," River stated. "Hey, look...I need to get back to work. I'll check in with you tomorrow."

He disconnected with Kenny and called Nova, unsure why he couldn't shake the worry that clung to him. "I just wanted to make sure you're all right and see if you needed anything."

"I'm fine." Her calm voice reassured him, but he could hear the exhaustion. "I ate something and took my medication."

"Okay," River said, trying to sound casual. "Call or text me if you need me to pick up dinner or something."

"I will. Thanks."

After hanging up, he stretched out on the bed, his body feeling out of sync with the time difference. As he lay there, thoughts of Nova filled his mind. He tried to find comfort in shifting from one side to the other, but it was useless.

Giving up on sleep after an hour of restlessness, River sat up in bed and propped himself against the pillows. He returned to reviewing the files on Mateo, but they couldn't distract him from the nagging thoughts about Nova and their complicated past.

CLAD IN A sports bra and a pair of leggings, Nova sat down on the edge of her king-size bed. She pulled her golden-brown hair into a high ponytail before sliding under the covers. The headache was now a dull throb.

At 3:07 p.m. her phone rang, the ringtone identifying the caller as her best friend.

She sat up in bed to take the call. "Hey, Jersey…"

"You all right?" she asked. "River told me what happened."

"River called *you*?" Nova couldn't believe it.

"Yeah. I was listed as your emergency contact. He had called the precinct the day everything happened and left a message for me. I was working a case and didn't call him back until a few minutes ago. He told me you were home now. How are you feeling?"

"I'm good," Nova responded.

"Girl, what happened?"

"I went to check on my witness, and someone clocked me good," she responded. "River was meeting me there. He found me unconscious."

"Thank goodness he showed up in time," Jersey said. "I think it's interesting that you are working together again."

Nova didn't respond.

"Do you need anything? I just got off work, but I can pick up something for you to eat."

"River called not too long ago asking if I needed anything. I told him I was good. I can always have something delivered."

"That was sweet of him."

"Yeah. Don't read too much into it, Jersey."

"Well, reach out if you change your mind. I can run out and pick you up something."

"I probably won't be bothering you," Nova said. "I'm going to take a nap."

"Check in with me when you wake up."

"Okay," Nova responded.

As she settled under her soft, fluffy comforter, Nova reached over and placed her smartphone on the nightstand.

She sighed in relief, hoping that the darkness and stillness of the room would help ease her pounding headache.

Just as she closed her eyes, the shrill ringtone of her work phone broke through the silence. Her hand darted to grab it.

"Deputy Marshal Bennett speaking," she answered professionally. But all she heard on the other end was silence.

"Who is this?" Nova asked, growing suspicious and slightly irritated.

Still, no response came from the other end, just an eerie quiet that sent a chill down her spine. "Arya?"

The caller hung up.

Nova bolted upright and called the office to ask one of the techs to trace the call.

She released a short sigh of frustration, abandoning the idea of a nap. She couldn't afford to be down right now.

Headache or not, she was going back to work.

The only reason she'd tried to rest was because her boss had insisted. Her gut instinct told her that Arya had been the caller.

"Where are you, Arya?" she whispered.

Rubbing her temples, Nova reached for her phone and dialed the office to check on the progress of the trace. As she listened to the ringing, her mind wandered back to the missing woman.

"Deputy Marshal Bennett, we managed to trace the call." An agent's voice crackled through the receiver, snapping Nova back to reality. Her heart raced as she leaned forward, anticipation filling her. "It's from a burner phone."

"Where did it come from?"

"It's strange. The call was traced back to an abandoned house in Concord."

So, Arya's still in North Carolina.

"Send the location to my phone, please."

"Sending now."

Without hesitation, Nova got out of bed. She slipped a hoodie over her head and grabbed her keys, determined to find Arya and bring her back into the safety of WITSEC.

Chapter Five

As Nova approached the abandoned house, her heart quickened with unease. The air was thick and still, almost as if it held its breath in anticipation. In the distance, she could hear the faint whispers of the trees rustling in the wind, adding to the ominous atmosphere.

She scanned the wooded area, searching for any signs of life, but there was nothing—no cars on the street, no movement behind the windows.

Taking a deep breath, Nova exited her car and stepped onto the cracked pavement. With each step closer to the house, she could feel a strange energy enveloping her, making her skin prickle with goose bumps. She'd considered calling River, but decided to venture out alone. Her thoughts were centered on Arya and finding her.

The front door hung open, the lock broken and swinging on its hinges. She couldn't tell if someone had forced it open or if time had slowly eroded its strength.

Cautiously, she entered the darkened interior. "Arya?" she called out softly. "It's me, Nova. Please don't be scared. I want to help you. I can take you somewhere safe." Her voice echoed through the empty halls, but there was no response except for the creaking of floorboards beneath her feet.

As Nova ventured farther into the house, the atmosphere grew even more suffocating. The air seemed to thicken, making it harder to breathe. The dying light from the outside filtered through the cracks in the boarded-up windows, casting eerie shadows on the peeling wallpaper.

With each step, Nova's apprehension deepened and her temples throbbed. A shiver danced down her spine, and she wrapped her arms around herself for comfort, though it offered little solace.

The silence was deafening, broken only by the distant howl of a neighborhood dog. As Nova ascended the creaky staircase, she felt a strange pull drawing her toward a particular room. The door stood slightly ajar, inviting her inside like a siren's call.

Summoning every ounce of courage, Nova placed her hand on her weapon before pushing open the door.

Evidence of recent occupancy was scattered about the bedroom. A brand-new sleeping bag lay crumpled on the floor, still bearing the crisp folds from its packaging. Empty fast-food containers and their greasy remnants were strewn on the dusty window seat, along with a roll of toilet paper and depleted water bottles. It was clear that someone had slept here, but they were long gone now.

This current setting before Nova was a stark contrast to the woman she had come to know. Arya de Leon was all about five-star hotels, often clutching the locket she wore around her neck at the thought of staying anywhere less extravagant.

Her gaze drifted back to the sleeping bag, and she strode over to it. With a nudge from her shoe, the cover was thrown open, revealing a cell phone inside. Nova was confident that it was the one used to call her earlier.

She hesitated for a moment, her mind racing with questions. Was it Arya who had left the phone here? And why?

Nova's curiosity got the better of her, compelling her to pick up the device. As she held it in her hand, the weight of intrigue settled upon her.

The screen flickered to life, displaying a simple text message: Find me.

RIVER WAS CAUGHT off guard when Nova reached out to him. He had offered to help with errands or bring food but never expected to actually hear from her.

"I heard from Arya," she announced.

"When?"

"She called me a couple of hours ago but didn't say anything."

"How did you know it was her?" he asked. "How can you be sure?"

"I wasn't until now," Nova responded. "I had a trace put on the number, which led to an old abandoned house in Concord. I followed the trail and—"

"You did *what*?" River's mind was abuzz as he took in the news. Nova had risked her safety and well-being to find answers, and he couldn't shake off his worry for her.

"I checked out the house and found the cell phone. There was a message on it that said, 'Find me.'"

"Nova, where are you right now?"

"I'm in my car at a gas station. I'm heading home when I hang up with you."

"Be safe."

"River, I'm fine. I feel fine."

As Nova promised to head back home, River couldn't shake off the conflicting emotions swirling inside him—relief and concern for Nova despite everything that had happened between them. He shouldn't care as much as he did.

As the minutes ticked by, River found himself pacing restlessly. Their shared history weighed heavily on his shoulders. Nova had vanished from his life once before, leaving him heartbroken and confused. The wounds from their past were still raw, yet she had managed to stir up a whirlwind of emotions within him once more.

A gentle breeze blew through the open balcony door, rustling the drapes and bringing a momentary respite to River's racing mind. As he gazed at the bustling city life below, nostalgia washed over him, reminding him of the two beautiful weeks he'd spent in Nova's embrace.

His mind strayed to Nova's mention of the message that was on the phone.

Find me.

The urgency in Arya's message echoed in his head, but a flicker of doubt crept in. Why flee again without speaking to Nova if she wanted to be found? Was that message really from Arya, or was something more insidious at play?

FIND ME.

With Mateo dead, Arya was now in the wind on her own. Nova considered that perhaps she was scared the intruder was on her trail, which may be why she continued to run. Nova couldn't rest until Arya was back safely. With the weight of her father's legacy on her shoulders, she couldn't afford to fail.

She had driven to the office to speak with Cohen and to drop off the phone after speaking with River. He agreed to send a team of agents to the abandoned house.

She planned to return to the Burlington house with River to attempt to retrace Arya's steps, searching for clues that could lead Nova to her whereabouts. She intended to scour the house, meticulously examining every corner, hoping to find a hidden message or hint pointing them in the right direction.

"We will find you," she vowed. Her father had never lost a witness, and she wouldn't either. This would not be her legacy.

Nova couldn't shake off the concern in River's voice during their brief phone call, but she couldn't afford to dwell on it either. Her priority was Arya and making sure she was safe. Yet a small part of her was grateful for his genuine worry despite their tension.

In solitude, Nova realized that it may not have been the most sensible choice to venture off to an abandoned house alone. But her determination to find Arya had driven her to take the risk. Unfortunately, she'd returned home without any luck in her search. She felt both aggravated and anxious for Arya's well-being.

As the sun continued dipping below the horizon, casting long shadows across the quiet street, the weight of Nova's unsuccessful search for Arya bore down on her shoulders, exacerbating her frustration and unease. The abandoned house loomed in her mind, haunting her thoughts with unanswered questions.

How did Arya come across the empty home? Why did she stay in North Carolina instead of seeking refuge with her parents? Am I reading this all wrong?

What if it was something more?

Her phone rang, cutting off her thoughts.

"I hope you're at home resting," River said when she answered.

"I am," Nova confirmed. "At least, my body is resting. My mind is busy trying to figure out this phone message.

Cohen's sending agents to watch the abandoned house. I'd like you and me to return to Mateo and Arya's home in the morning. I want us to conduct our own search."

"Sounds like a plan," River said. "Anything on her vehicle?"

"Not yet."

"Do you want to meet me at my hotel?"

"Just come to the Marshals office. I'll be there in the morning."

"Do you still have the phone?"

"No, I took it to the office. I want it checked for prints."

"I guess I'll see you in the morning."

"See you then," she murmured.

They hung up.

Nova had gotten out of bed and walked through her house while talking to him, checking locks and arming the security system. Arya was still at the forefront of her mind.

She had to find her before the cartel did, no matter what it took. Nothing would stop Nova from keeping Arya safe.

THE EARLY MORNING sun cast a soft glow over the quiet suburban neighborhood as Nova and River parked their vehicle discreetly down the street from the de Leons' residence. The house, surrounded by neatly trimmed hedges and a white picket fence, appeared calm and unassuming.

As Nova approached the porch, she noticed the once lush and vibrant ferns drooping and wilting from neglect. The leaves hung limply, their once bright green color faded to a dull, sickly shade. It was as if the plants were crying out for help. Nova made a mental note to give them the care and attention they deserved before they left the house.

She adjusted the strap of her holster as she approached the front door. River followed closely behind. They exchanged a quick nod before Nova knocked on the door, the sound echoing through the stillness of the morning.

No answer.

She pushed away the thought of what had happened the last time she was here. Nova's instincts kicked in, and she reached into her pocket for the spare key.

With a swift turn, the door creaked open, revealing a dimly lit living room.

The air inside was tense as they stepped into the house.

Nova swept her surroundings, her eyes scanning for any signs of disturbance or anything that seemed out of place.

They moved through the house methodically, checking every room for any clues or indications of where Arya might have gone. Nova examined the study, rifling through papers and files. River focused on the kitchen, checking the refrigerator and cabinets for any signs of sudden departure.

As they explored, a sense of urgency grew. The unanswered questions fueled their determination to find Arya before it was too late.

Nova halted in front of a corkboard behind the desk, covered with pictures and notes. She traced her finger over a recent photograph of Arya, reminding herself of the stakes involved.

River discovered a plastic bag hidden between packages of meat in the freezer. "Nova, take a look at this," he called, holding up a small notebook he found inside.

The notebook contained cryptic notes and coded messages, hinting at Mateo's attempts to stay one step ahead of the cartel and law enforcement.

Nova's eyes narrowed as she scanned the pages, noting the dates and realizing that Mateo had been preparing for something all along.

"He never intended to stay in WITSEC," she told River. "He had money stashed in several banks in other countries."

"Looks like he never intended to testify. He and Arya were going to leave the country."

"We really need to find her," Nova said, determination flashing in her eyes.

With newfound purpose, Nova and River continued their search, determined to unravel the mystery surrounding Arya de Leon's disappearance and bring her back to safety.

The morning sun climbed higher in the sky, casting a determined light on their path as they pursued the elusive trail that would lead them to Arya's whereabouts.

LATER IN THE DAY, River went to the local DEA agency to check out a few things and to reconnect with a friend he'd met years ago when they attended college.

"I heard you were in town," Taylor said. "I was out yesterday when you called."

"They told me that you called in sick. You all right?"

"Yep, I'm great. My son was the one who was sick. He's getting over a stomach virus. My wife had to be in court yesterday, so I had to stay home and clean up the messes from both ends. Man, I'm traumatized."

River chuckled. "Poor you…"

Shaking his head, Taylor said, "You don't know the half of it."

They walked into the break room for coffee.

"So, what brings you to Charlotte? And where is your partner?"

"Kenny's back home working our investigation on that end," River said. "I came here because one of my witnesses is dead and another is missing."

"Any leads?"

"Not very many, but we're exploring all of them. I need a space to work."

"There's an empty desk behind me," Taylor offered. "You can plug in your computer there."

"Thanks."

River added copies of the information they found at the house to his file. He called his partner and discussed his findings. He and Nova weren't sure whether Arya was still in town, but there was no doubt that she would turn up in San Diego at some point.

Sunlight filtered through the blinds and lent an air of secrecy to his solitary pursuit. Every document, every line of text he scrutinized brought him closer to uncovering Mateo's slipup.

As time ticked by, River's anticipation ignited like a flame in the depths of his chest. A strong sense of determination coursed through his veins, driving him to unravel and destroy Mateo's intricate schemes of corruption. Despite the fact that their key witness was deceased, his information could still shed light on the inner workings of the drug cartel.

As River carefully examined the financial records, a peculiar pattern emerged. It seemed that Mateo had unknowingly left a trail—an intricate breadcrumb trail leading straight to his betrayal.

River's eyes widened with astonishment as he connected the dots, realizing that Mateo's slipup was not just a simple miscalculation but a meticulously calculated move to divert attention from his true motives.

As he delved deeper into the financial records, River's analytical mind pieced together the irregularities that had initially caught his attention. It was a web of intricate transactions, money funneled through various shell companies and offshore accounts. The path seemed convoluted at first, but patterns emerged; hidden beneath the facade of legitimate business dealings lay a complex network of bribery and embezzlement.

Still, there were gaps in the information. There were more, perhaps critical details on the cartel's business dealings that Mateo hadn't shared. The cartel's operations extended far beyond what he had revealed, and River was determined to uncover the truth.

He leaned back in his chair, his mind racing with possibilities. He reached for his coffee, taking a slow sip as he considered his next move.

Some of the handwritten entries were written by someone else. River assumed that Arya was the writer. Although he hadn't met them, his gut told him that the only person Mateo would've trusted with this information was his wife. If his theory was correct, then this was proof that Arya knew of her husband's relationship with the cartel.

He pulled out his phone and tapped out a message, fingers moving rapidly over the screen.

Can you meet me in thirty minutes? River sent the text to Nova, hoping she would agree to see him.

Sure. My place okay? came the reply.

Yes. He slipped his phone into his jeans pocket.

River took his time gathering his notes, making sure they were organized. He spent a few more minutes catching up with Taylor before heading out to his car.

River knew that Nova had more information about Arya than he did. He depended on her knowledge; they would have to work together to find the missing woman.

The lingering recollections of their ill-fated romance, the repercussions from their previous joint assignment, weighed heavily in the atmosphere, forming an uneasy knot in River's stomach. He desperately wanted to keep things strictly professional.

River pulled into the driveway and turned off the car's engine.

Nova was waiting for him by the front door, and she stepped aside to let him enter the foyer. "What's going on?" she asked.

"I just finished going through Mateo's file," River replied. "He gave us some useful information, but as I followed the trail, I'm convinced that he didn't give us everything. Considering his position, every financial transaction was done with his knowledge."

"I believe you," Nova said. "Their house had been searched— someone was looking for something. Apparently, they didn't find anything on Mateo when they killed him."

"He could've stored it somewhere safe, or he gave it to Arya," River stated. "I also found some handwritten entries that I believe were written by a woman."

"You think it was Arya?"

He nodded. "I do."

Nova eyed him. "Either way, she's not safe."

Their gazes locked, both understanding the urgency and danger that surrounded them. "That's why we have to find her," River declared, determination evident in his voice.

"Right now, all we have is a cell phone," Nova stated.

"What about the place where you found the phone?" River asked. "I would think that's where we'll find clues. The first of which is the phone—she knew you'd be able to trace the location. That's most likely why she called you and stayed on the line."

"The house was searched and nothing else was found," she announced. "The sleeping bag was taken into evidence, along with the food containers. There wasn't anything else there."

"There's only one way to find out for sure," River said. "Up for a drive?"

"Always. But it's going to be dark soon."

"I have a couple of flashlights."

Nova's cell rang.

She answered it.

He heard her utter a word of profanity. The call wasn't good news.

She ended the call, saying, "Arya's SUV was just found in a Target parking lot. They searched the stores in the shopping center. She's nowhere to be found."

Inside the car, River asked, "How is your head?"

"I'm good," Nova answered.

They parked down the street from the house in Concord and waited.

"How did she even find this place?" he wondered aloud.

"I have no idea," Nova responded. "I can't imagine her staying behind in North Carolina."

"Maybe that was part of Mateo's plan," he suggested.

She nodded in agreement. "So, what do you think? Should we head inside?"

"Let's do it."

The air was heavy with anticipation as they approached the dilapidated structure. The moon's feeble glow offered little visibility, casting eerie shadows upon each broken windowpane.

To River, the house stood as a forgotten relic of a bygone era, its secrets buried within its decaying walls.

Nova led him up to the bedroom on the second floor. "This is where I found the phone."

The sleeping bag was gone, but the rotting remains of

old take-out containers filled the room with a sour odor. She wrinkled her nose in disgust.

River glanced around the room with observant eyes. The walls were cracked and peeling, with remnants of old wallpaper clinging on for dear life.

"I told you that there's nothing here," Nova uttered in frustration. "Right now, all we have is a message on a phone."

"It's a start," he said. "Were there any other calls made?"

"No. It only had my number."

"Then she must have another burner," River suggested. "My partner is still surveilling her parents' home. No sighting of Arya as of yet."

Nova eyed him. "What do you think about flying out to San Diego? I think we should speak to Pablo and Ramona Lozano in person. There's a chance that Arya's on her way there. We'll check flights, but my gut tells me that she will most likely travel by car."

River hesitated a brief second before replying, "I understand your drive to see this through, but you need to consult with your doctor first. Changes in air pressure and cabin conditions during a flight could affect you after the concussion."

"I can't just sit around and wait for something to happen!" Nova snapped, her hands clenching into fists at her sides.

"I'm not saying you can't travel," River reassured her, his voice firm but gentle. "But we need to be cautious."

"I understand your concern, River," Nova said through gritted teeth, trying to rein in her impatience. "But Arya needs our help."

River watched Nova fidget with the hem of her linen shirt, a determined furrow in her brow. He could sense the familiar blaze of determination burning within her, but he also knew that caution was necessary in this situation. With Arya still on the loose, pushing Nova to take it easy was impossible.

Chapter Six

Nova wasn't interested in seeing her doctor. She was more than capable of taking care of herself. She didn't want someone telling her that she was grounded because she'd had a minor concussion. She intended to be on the plane with River heading to San Diego despite this. Arya had been missing for three days now, and Nova couldn't bear the thought of the woman being out there alone and in danger.

As she packed her bag with essentials for the journey, Nova felt a mix of anticipation and anxiety. She knew that finding Arya wouldn't be an easy task, but she was willing to go to any lengths to bring her home safely.

River, always the voice of reason, watched Nova with concern. "Are you sure about this?" he asked, his brow furrowing. "Your health is important, too, you know."

"I'll be fine." She brushed off his worries with a dismissive wave of her hand. "Besides, we can't just sit around and wait for something to happen. Arya needs us."

He openly studied her.

"I'm fine, River. You need to go back to the hotel and pack," Nova stated. "I want to be on the first flight out tomorrow." She sat down on the sofa and picked up her cell phone. "I need to call Cohen."

After speaking with her supervisor and assuring him

that she was fine, he backed River's suggestion to see her doctor.

She hung up and scheduled a video visit with her physician. Thirty minutes later, they discussed her travel plans.

"No headaches," Nova said. "No problem with my vision. I feel good."

When the appointment ended, River approached her cautiously, worry evident in his eyes. "Your health is more important than finding Arya right this moment. I'll be searching for her and we can get other agents on this case."

Nova looked up at him, a fire burning in her eyes. "You don't understand," she replied, her voice laced with determination. "Arya is my witness. I'm responsible for her. I can't just sit back and do nothing while she's out there, possibly in danger. I have to find her."

"All right." He nodded resignedly. "Your doctor didn't have a problem with it, and I can't stop you. Just promise me that you won't push yourself too hard."

Nova paused for a moment, contemplating River's words. She realized that he was right. She couldn't let her determination blind her to the importance of her well-being. Taking a deep breath, she said, "I promise," her voice softer now, filled with gratitude for his concern. "I won't push myself too hard, and I'll make sure to look after myself as we search for Arya."

River prepared to leave.

"I'll see you tomorrow at the airport," Nova said.

He stepped out, and she watched him get into the rental and disappear from the city streets.

As night fell, Nova was consumed by a whirlwind of emotions. The weight of uncertainty pressed down on her chest, but she refused to let it deter her from finding Arya.

She knew that time was of the essence, and every moment spent apart was another moment Arya could be in danger.

RIVER ARRIVED BACK at his hotel room shortly after 9:00 p.m. He and Taylor had eaten dinner across the street from the DEA agency on Randolph Road.

He was about to shower when his phone began to vibrate. He picked it up off the marble counter. "Hello."

He walked out of the bathroom and sat down on the edge of the bed.

"Hey, big brother."

A smile tugged at his lips. Despite his feelings about their mother, he shared a special bond with his sister. "Bonnie, how are you?"

"I'm okay. I'd like to know what's going on with you. I haven't heard a word from you since Mama's funeral."

River sank into a nearby chair. "I've been busy with work."

"She's been gone almost six months."

His jaw tightened. "I know."

"Do you think you'll ever forgive her?"

"I forgave Mary a long time ago, Bonnie." River had always addressed his mother by her first name. Mary was more like a sister. No, not even that. Mary was more of an acquaintance.

"She was sixteen when she had you, River. At that time, Mama didn't know anything about being a mother."

"I've heard it all before and I'm fine," he responded. "You don't have to worry about me."

"But I do worry. I know you feel like Mama abandoned you. I know she didn't raise you, but you were always in her heart."

"That's exactly what she did. None of it matters now."

River didn't want to talk about the effect his mother's rejection had had on him.

He was the result of his teen mother's relationship with an older boy who went off to college and never returned home. She'd never told anyone his name—just moved on with her life and without her son.

He swallowed hard, forcing down the bitterness that threatened to spill out.

"After Mama got married and had me, she wanted to get you, but Grandma wouldn't let her take you. She told Mama that you were more her son than anyone else's."

That was a lie. He'd heard his grandmother practically beg her daughter to raise him with his sister. Mary had flat out refused. She'd told her mother that she didn't want a boy, but River didn't want to hurt Bonnie with the truth. His sister adored Mary. "Bonnie, all I can say is that the damage was done long before then. Look, I can't unfeel the way I felt growing up without Mary's love. Like I said earlier…it doesn't matter anymore."

"I miss you, River."

"When I can get some free time, I'll make a trip to Sacramento to visit with you," he said.

"I hope you mean it."

"Bonnie, I mean every word. I'll call you and check in next week. I promise." Despite his feelings for their mother, River never let them affect his relationship with Bonnie, who was eight years younger. He loved his sister beyond measure.

He buried his emotions deep within himself, pushing away any thoughts of Mary and Nova. The painful rejections from both women still lingered in his mind, but River had a mission to focus on.

Finding Arya de Leon was his top priority, no matter

how much his heart ached for the love he had lost. He couldn't afford to let these distractions hinder him, not when so much was at stake.

River pushed aside the pain and focused solely on the task at hand, determined to succeed no matter the cost.

THE NEXT MORNING, Nova continued to try to contact Arya several times at the cell number she'd been issued by WITSEC. She arrived at the airport and met River at their gate, hoping that Arya had gone to her parents' house and they could speak to her soon. However, when Nova had called the Lozanos last evening, Pablo and Ramona denied their daughter was there. They both claimed they hadn't spoken to her in years.

The steady hum of airport activity surrounded Nova as she stared at her laptop screen, her eyes skimming words without registering their meaning. Frustration gnawed at her, a relentless companion echoing the turmoil within. She couldn't shake the feeling that the threads of Arya's disappearance were slipping through her fingers like grains of sand.

Beside her, River's silence mirrored the weight of the unsaid.

An electric current seemed to crackle between them, unspoken and undeniable. As Nova's fingers grazed the rough surface of her laptop, she could feel River's intense gaze piercing through her, causing her jaw to clench with unease. With a quick snap, she shut out the outside world, wanting desperately to escape the heavy tension that hung in the air. But even in this momentary respite, she couldn't shake off the powerful pull that River had on her.

Their boarding announcement echoed through the intercom, and Nova stood up, her movements precise, purposeful toward the gate agent. This journey held more than the promise of flight—it was a pursuit of answers.

The agent, indifferent to the weight of their mission, processed the documents with routine efficiency.

As they took their seats on the plane, the engines hummed to life, drowning out the doubts in Nova's mind. Leaning back, she glanced at River, their eyes locking in a silent pact. The aircraft taxied down the runway, hurtling them further into their investigation.

The plane transported Nova and River into the unknown, leaving their unresolved tension in the air like the turbulence that awaited them.

THE SCENT LINGERED, a ghost haunting River's senses with every breath. If only she hadn't worn that perfume. It wrapped around him like a relentless adversary, an uninvited companion on this mission. River's attempts to ignore it proved futile, each whiff a reminder of a vulnerability he wasn't prepared to acknowledge.

In the cramped confines of the plane, River fought to regain control. He couldn't afford distraction, not now. Not when the stakes were so high.

As Nova excused herself to make a phone call, River took a moment to collect himself. Leaning back in his seat, he closed his eyes.

"I can't let her affect me this way," he muttered, a vow to steel himself against the unseen forces at play. "I'm in control."

But as the minutes ticked away, doubts crept in like shadows. Was he truly in control, or was it a facade he clung to for pride? The truth whispered in the recesses of his mind, a nagging reminder that emotions were not easily subdued. As the flight wore on, the plane's hum became a backdrop to the internal struggle within River. He opened his eyes, glancing toward the empty seat beside him where Nova would soon return. The air still carried faint traces of her presence, a reminder that she held an inexplicable sway over him.

A sense of vulnerability gnawed at him. In this clandestine battle of wills, it became evident that the only person in control was Nova. The realization settled over him and River grappled with the unsettling truth—he was navigating uncharted territory. The compass of his emotions pointed directly toward her.

If only she hadn't worn that perfume. It was the one he remembered on her from their two weeks together, when he'd felt the rush of falling for her. He'd been so certain that feeling would last. After the heart-wrenching pain and betrayal he'd experienced the first time, River knew he couldn't risk opening his heart to Nova again. The thought of being vulnerable and potentially getting hurt once more was enough to send shivers down his spine. He couldn't bear the thought of going through that kind of agony again, and losing her a second time would surely break him beyond repair. No, it was safer for him to keep his heart guarded, even if it meant sacrificing the possibility of a future with Nova.

I can't let her affect me this way, he thought silently. *I won't let her do this to me. I'm in control.*

Was he, really? Because the way River felt right now… The only person in control was Nova.

Chapter Seven

Nova didn't relish having to endure the cloud of uneasiness surrounding them for the next five and a half hours. They had all this quiet time together to clear the air... It was time to tell him exactly how she felt. She cleared her throat. "I know things between us are strained, but I thought we could coexist. We're working a case. This isn't some social outing. We're supposed to be a *team* on this investigation. I don't have a problem working with you, but can you say the same about me? Because if you can't, then you need to just have the case reassigned to another agent."

"That won't be necessary," River responded. "I can manage my feelings while working with you, Nova."

"I apologize," she said. "I guess I'm letting my personal feelings affect my judgment and it was unprofessional. It won't happen again." Nova rubbed the right side of her temple, trying to massage away the hint of a headache. It was a subtle reminder that she'd suffered a concussion.

"I'm sorry if I haven't been my professional self either," he said.

Nova nodded, satisfied with where they'd left things. She took an aspirin and checked her emails. Then she settled in her seat and closed her eyes as she waited for the pill to work its magic.

"I don't remember you ever being this quiet."

She opened her eyes and looked at River. "I have a lot on my mind."

"Is this the first witness to do a disappearing act on you?"

"Yeah," she said. "And hopefully my last. I know that most of the people in the program are criminals and that they often struggle with what they perceive as mundane living. Some have difficulty leaving their previous life behind and often return to old habits. I know now that I was right to be concerned about Mateo."

"From everything I've learned about him, Mateo was a greedy man," River said. "He wouldn't have been happy with a simple life in some small town."

Nova couldn't disagree because River spoke the truth. Mateo was an intelligent man who'd decided to apply his accounting expertise to aid the cartel in cheating the government of tax dollars and helped them launder drug money.

She'd been a case agent for Mateo for the past eight months. Before that, Nova had worked a six-month protection detail for a federal judge who had been receiving death threats.

She stole a peek at River, who seemed interested in an in-flight movie. She pulled her iPad out and opened a book to read. She almost released an audible sigh of relief when the headache finally surrendered to nothingness.

THEY WALKED IN silence through airport exit doors to pick up their rental—Nova had chosen an SUV—and drove out of the parking lot ten minutes later.

"It's been quite a while since I was here in San Diego," she said, programming the Lozanos' address into her GPS. "Probably five years or so."

"I came down for a conference a couple of months ago," River responded.

Pointing to her left, Nova asked, "Hey, are you still crazy about In-N-Out?"

His expression suddenly became animated as he said, "I *love* In-N-Out. You know that's my spot."

Grinning, Nova maneuvered the vehicle into the drive-through line. They'd skipped breakfast and might as well eat on the way. They placed their orders and then pulled out into traffic again.

"How much do Arya's parents know about her situation?" River asked when they'd finished eating.

"They were allowed to say goodbye before they went into the program. So, they know she's in WITSEC. From day one, it was made clear that she wasn't to have any contact with them."

"That knowledge alone could get them killed," River said.

"I know."

He glimpsed the worried expression on Nova's face.

Glancing over at him, she said, "I hate that this is happening on my watch."

"Don't take it personally."

"It's hard not to do so," she retorted. "They got on my nerves more than once, but I wanted to see them thrive in this new life. Not everyone gets a second chance, you know..."

River nodded in agreement. "They have to want it for themselves, Nova."

"I know you're right." Her mind was working overtime as she tried to figure out Arya's next move.

"We're going to find her."

Nova gave him a grateful smile as she tried to ignore the cold knot in her stomach.

River saw Nova massaging her right temple. "Do you have a headache? Why don't you let me drive?"

"No, I'm good. We're almost to our destination."

Five minutes later, Nova pulled into the neighborhood. She put the vehicle in Park at the top of the street and turned off the ignition. Her eyes bounced around, searching.

He glanced around, too.

"Who are you looking for?" she asked.

"I wanted to see if one of our guys was still on surveillance," River responded. "Must have taken a break."

Nova finished off her bottled water.

He pointed straight ahead. "That's the house over there."

"There aren't any lights on," she observed aloud as she looked in the direction he was pointing. "You think they go to bed this early?"

"Nope," River stated. "The last time they were spotted was about a day ago. No one has been in or out since then. My partner said that they don't venture out much."

Nova got out of the car and slipped on a Kevlar vest.

"What are you doing?" he asked.

"I can't explain it, but I have a bad feeling about this. I felt this same way in Burlington." She already had her weapon in hand. She wasn't going to let anyone jump her a second time. "We need to make sure they're okay."

River followed suit, putting on his own vest, then walked behind her as she approached the back of the house. "Look at the back door," Nova said in a loud whisper. "Someone broke in."

She tried the knob, turning it gently. "It's unlocked."

Nova pulled out her phone and called the police before going inside.

They entered the house gingerly.

River tried a light switch.

Nothing.

Nova found the darkness thick and claustrophobic. It was like a hand closing around her throat. She pulled out a miniature flashlight.

"The power's been cut off," he said.

With her flashlight, Nova's eyes bounced around her surroundings. When she walked into the living room, she said, "I seriously doubt that Mr. and Mrs. Lozano left their house looking like this. We can safely assume that this house has been ransacked."

River nodded in agreement. "It looks like a crime scene."

"Do you think they've been kidnapped?" she asked.

He pointed upstairs. "It's possible. There's a packed suitcase up there that was probably left by mistake. They have security cameras in place throughout the house but the wires have been cut. I noticed it when I checked the garage."

"That's just great..." Nova walked back into the living room and was about to ascend the staircase.

A knock sounded on the front door.

"Is it the police?" Nova asked.

"Naw, it looks like he might be a neighbor," River said, peeking out of the front window.

"I came to see what's going on over here," a middle-aged man with a trim beard said when Nova opened the door.

She showed him her badge. "You took great risk coming over here after noting strangers in the house," she chided. "What if I weren't law enforcement? You could've been killed."

"I thought you were the police," he replied. "The people that own this place left town. Pablo called and told me that they were going away for a couple of weeks. He sounded scared." He looked past River. "What's going on over here?"

"Looks like there might have been a break-in," Nova said. "Did you happen to see anyone else near the house?"

"I never saw anyone outside of Pablo and Ramona, other than Yolanda, their housekeeper."

Nova and River exchanged looks. "I'm sorry, but I have to go back inside," he said. "Thank you for your help."

"Jerry Spotswood. That's my name." The man stepped off the porch and River swung the door closed.

Nova rushed up the stairs with River following close behind.

They proceeded cautiously through the house, their senses heightened by the ominous atmosphere that clung to the air.

With a shared nod, they approached the door of a room, the creaking floorboards beneath their feet betraying their presence. Pushing the door open slowly, they revealed a dimly lit guest bedroom. The space was a tableau of horror.

Their eyes fell upon Yolanda, her lifeless body slumped in the corner. Blood pooled around her, staining the white carpet a dark red. Nova and River entered, their guns drawn as they cautiously scanned the area for an intruder.

Then Nova rushed to Yolanda's side, checking for a pulse she knew wasn't there. Her heart sank as she realized they were too late.

Turning to River, she could see the same anger and determination she felt in his eyes. An innocent woman was dead, but they would not rest until they found those responsible.

As they combed through the room for evidence, Nova noticed a glint of metal under Yolanda's hand. Pulling back the woman's fingers, she discovered a small piece of jewelry engraved with a strange symbol.

River's voice broke through her thoughts. "We need to call this in. The killers can't be far."

But Nova couldn't shake the image of Yolanda's terror-filled eyes from her mind. She vowed to get justice for the woman, no matter what it took. "They didn't have to kill her."

"Johnny Boy doesn't believe in leaving witnesses behind," River responded, pulling out his phone. "I need to call my partner. I don't know what happened here, so I'm hoping he can help me make sense of this."

In the living room, she looked at the photos lining the walls and the mantel over the fireplace, paying close attention to the picturesque details. There were several framed photos of a house with mountains in the backdrop. Nova grabbed a few. She hoped they might explain where Arya and her parents may be hiding.

"Jerry lives across the street," River said. "I had Kenny check him out. He's been living there for the past ten years. As far as we can tell, he has no cartel connections."

"Was he able to explain what happened with the surveillance?" Nova asked.

"There was a disconnect. The team was taken off prematurely. My supervisor isn't happy right now. This is on us."

"It looks like Arya's parents packed in a hurry to me," Nova observed as she continued looking around. "But why? Is it because she warned them, or were they hurrying to get to her?"

"It could be both," River responded.

"But killing her parents won't force Arya out of hiding," Nova said.

"But it could *silence* her forever," he said. "It could make her too afraid to ever speak against them."

She nodded in agreement.

Nova could sense the frustration written all over River's face. She understood that it was weighing on him that the surveillance team had been abruptly removed from Arya's parents and now the housekeeper had been killed.

They heard the shrill scream of sirens in the distance.

Nova and River stood on the corner, watching the flashing lights approach. Whirring sirens grew louder, piercing the calm suburban ambience like a discordant melody.

Moments later, Jerry appeared, hastily jogging toward them with his trusty flashlight. His face etched with concern, he seemed to age before their eyes. His neatly trimmed beard was now disheveled, and sweat glistened on his furrowed brow.

Jerry abruptly stopped beside Nova and River. "What in the world is going on? I've been patrolling these streets for years—nothing has ever happened in this neighborhood… Well, just some teens wreaking havoc."

Nova laid a gentle hand on Jerry's trembling shoulder. "Yolanda's dead."

He gasped in shock. "I never heard a thing."

Minutes ticked by like hours as they waited in silence.

The flashing lights of the approaching police cars grew brighter, casting an eerie glow upon the once peaceful street. Neighbors began peering out the windows and leaving their houses, drawn by the commotion.

"This neighborhood will never be the same," Jerry uttered.

"I THINK WE should hang back and watch the house to see if someone comes back tonight," River said after the police and CSI team left. He wanted to catch the perpetrator who had taken an innocent life, but he also knew that the surveillance team had probably been pulled due to budget cuts. Should they take a chance and stay back to see if anyone returned to the crime scene? "It's a long shot, but that's all we have right now." He stood outside the vehicle, watching.

Nova nodded in agreement. "Let's do it."

It was after 10:00 p.m. It was just dark enough on the street to provide some cover for the surveillance. River had positioned the rental car well away from the house but close enough to see if anyone drove up. The view was excellent but discreet enough for them to keep from being seen.

Now and then, they caught movement in one of the windows at Jerry's house. He was watching the empty home as well.

"I still don't believe Arya knows anything about her husband's business dealings."

"Nova, she may not be as innocent as you'd like to think," River said, not understanding why she had so much faith in Mateo's wife. "I watched Arya's interview, and her answers sounded rehearsed to me, but I don't know the woman."

"Arya was probably nervous," Nova explained. "Her whole life was changing in a short period."

He opened the driver's-side door for Nova.

"Thanks," she murmured.

River walked to the other side of the car and got in.

"Do you really think Arya's parents plan to return to this house?" Nova asked.

"I'm not sure, but you'd think by now they know something's wrong," River responded. "Like the fact that their alarm isn't working. I'm sure the alarm company has tried to reach them. If they're not running, why not come home?"

"We can assume that Arya warned them, which is why they left town. We need to find them all. I don't want any more bodies turning up."

"I don't want that either," he said. River hoped that Arya's parents would be found alive and well.

Staring out the driver's window, Nova stated, "I really hope Arya's with her parents. If she isn't, then I don't know where to begin looking for her." She wanted to roll down the window so the breeze could wrap itself around her like a soft shawl on a cool evening. "We didn't really have any reason to think they were in danger. With Mateo dead, I can't figure why they'd want Arya or her parents."

He looked over at her. "The cartel isn't going to give up."

"I know," she responded with a sigh.

"Nova, whatever happens…this isn't on you," River said.

"That's what everyone says, but the facts are that Mateo and Arya went missing on my watch. I was responsible for them. If something worse happens and fingers are pointed, they'll be at *me*."

He could tell that Nova was taking this to heart. She was great at her job and dedicated to keeping her witnesses safe. River didn't want to see her begin to doubt herself. *That's when people start to make mistakes.*

Chapter Eight

Nova was becoming antsy just sitting in the car doing nothing. Her mind was all over the place. If Arya wasn't in San Diego, then where could she be?

Anywhere.

She bit her bottom lip, trying to remember if Arya had ever mentioned anything that would explain her whereabouts. The woman had often griped about living in North Carolina and openly expressed her desire to return to her life in Los Angeles.

"Do you think she would risk returning to LA like her husband did?" Nova posed the question.

River replied, "It's worth considering. At this point, we can't rule out any possibilities."

"I know a couple of people we should talk to—they might be able to help us," Nova said. "There's Kaleb Stone, a close friend of my father's. The night my dad was killed, he stepped in to provide security for a cartel witness determined to return home. He was on his way to the safe house... My dad had been shot... He was dead by the time Kaleb arrived."

"I actually know Kaleb. The last time I saw him was right after he left the Marshals."

"He opened his own security firm after he left."

"So, what happened to the witness?" River asked.

"He married her," Nova responded with a chuckle. "After she testified against Calderon and a few other high-ranking members of the cartel."

"Are you talking about the Homeland Security agent who was shot at with her partner a few years ago? Everybody thought she'd died, too."

"Yeah."

"So, she left WITSEC to go back to LA?"

Nova nodded. "There was a leak in the Milwaukee office. It was a mess, but after that, the Marshals changed some of the protocols regarding witness security. But now I'm wondering if we have a leak here. I'm still trying to figure out how they found the house in Burlington."

River settled back in his seat. "We are aware that Poppy and Johnny Boy were using bribery and blackmail to control individuals within various levels of law enforcement and the government. But there is a chance they obtained information by killing Mateo. His body was found without any identification, so it's possible they had accomplices visit his house."

"That's why I think we should talk to Kaleb and Rylee. They've been investigating the Mancuso cartel for the past two years," Nova said. "Since we're here in California, it won't hurt to meet with them."

"I'm open to it," River said. "Without Mateo alive to testify and if Arya doesn't have any information…my case against the cartel will fall apart. I don't want that to happen on my watch."

Nova placed a call to Kaleb Stone. "Hey, it's me. I'm in San Diego."

"Nova, hi. How long will you be here?"

"A few days," she responded. "If you and Rylee aren't

busy, I'd love for you two to come down. I want your feedback on a case I'm working with the DEA. It's concerning the Mancuso cartel."

"Rylee and I can fly down there tomorrow morning. I'll text you once I make the flight arrangements."

"Thanks a lot, Kaleb."

"I'll see you tomorrow."

Nova hung up, saying, "They're flying down in the morning to see us." She glanced around, then said, "I don't know about you, but I'm not looking forward to sleeping in this car."

"A couple of agents should be arriving soon to take over surveillance," River said. "We can head to the hotel when they get here."

The mention of a hotel reminded Nova of a similar situation two years ago. They'd been tracking a fugitive. The more time they'd spent together, the harder they'd found it to ignore their growing attraction, so they gave in to their feelings. Two weeks later, Nova had walked out of his life the day after they'd apprehended the guy.

"You okay?" he asked, cutting into her thoughts.

"Huh... Yeah, I'm good."

After the agents arrived, River had a brief discussion with them before he and Nova left the area. "There's a hotel not too far from here," he announced.

"That's fine," Nova replied. "As long as they have a comfy bed, I can sleep anywhere."

"I only stay at a certain hotel brand," River said.

She smiled. "You sound like Mateo and his wife."

River eyed her. "Are you saying that you don't have a favorite chain?"

"I do, but I'm also open to staying elsewhere."

They settled on any hotel under the Marriott brand.

Nova pulled into the first one that came up on the GPS. "This is the Mission Valley location."

"I'm fine with that," River said. "I've stayed here once before. It's very nice inside."

"I'm good with clean and comfortable," she said. "After a few hours' sleep, I'll be ready to return to work."

RIVER'S STOMACH COMPLAINED loudly enough to garner Nova's attention. "Sorry about that," he said.

She gave a tiny smile. "You're not alone. I'm hungry, too."

They got out of the car after pulling into the hotel parking lot. River grabbed their luggage and followed behind Nova.

Inside the hotel, they checked into separate rooms.

"I'm going to grab a bite to eat," River announced in the elevator. "When I get back, we can try to create some type of timeline leading up to Arya's disappearance."

"I need to eat as well. Why don't we order room service?" Nova suggested. "This way, we can keep working over dinner."

He didn't respond as thoughts ran through his head. Room service... How many room service meals had they enjoyed two years ago? Intimate dinners that had led to him telling her things about his past, about his feelings, that he shouldn't have...

At River's hesitation, she said, "C'mon... It's just a meal. We should be mature enough to eat together."

He chided himself for reading too much into the situation. Nova wasn't trying to make dinner more than it appeared to be—she just wanted to continue working while they ate. River couldn't deny that it was the best use of their time. "We can do that," he relented.

Nova unlocked her door and held it open for him to enter.

"Where's the menu?" River asked, leaving his suitcase near the door. He placed hers right outside the closet.

She pointed to a thin binder on the desk. "It's over there." After they flipped through, Nova called to place their order. While they waited, she let her mind drift back to the Lozanos and where they could be. Had they lied when they'd said Arya hadn't contacted them recently? If she had, she could've put the cartel on her parents' trail.

A knock at the door interrupted her thoughts. She answered and took the meals from the hotel server. "The food's here," Nova announced as she brought them in. "Perfect timing, because I'm starving."

She placed a covered plate in front of River. "I can't believe you were so hungry and then you just ordered a salad and bread."

"It's late," he responded. "I don't sleep well after a heavy meal."

"Heavy or not, I'm going to enjoy my grilled salmon burger and fries. I'm not gonna feel guilty about it."

River chuckled. "I hear you. Enjoy your meal."

A mischievous grin on her face, Nova held out a french fry to him, saying, "Here... I know you want one."

"What are you trying to do?" He gave her a sidelong glance. "Tempt me?"

"I just remember how much you love a good fry."

"I'll pass," River said.

Nova's smile disappeared and she dropped her gaze to her plate.

The air in the room had abruptly become stuffy.

"You wanted to discuss the case," he said. River loaded salad onto his fork, clearly not wanting to lose focus.

She cleared her throat softly. "Yeah. Where do you want to start?"

"From the beginning. Has Arya ever mentioned a place she loved visiting? When a witness runs, they may go to someplace familiar to them."

"She wanted to be relocated to New York or Chicago— we decided they were the wrong places to send them." Nova stuck her french fry into a puddle of ketchup. "We felt the smaller the town, the better for them."

"Her parents travel a lot," River said. "They could be anywhere."

Nova nodded. "We should check hotels. They have to sleep sometime."

River chewed, considering, and she spotted the bread-crumbs that had gathered near the corner of his mouth. Without thinking, she reached out to brush them away. The action took her back to a time when he welcomed her touch.

He jerked his head back as if stung.

"Crumbs," she murmured. "Sorry."

River wiped his mouth with a napkin.

Embarrassed, Nova concentrated on her food and waited for the moment of awkwardness to become a thing of the past. She hoped River didn't get the wrong idea. It had been a stupid move on her part, although it wasn't planned.

Her phone emitted a sound, notifying her of an incoming text.

Nova read it, then said, "Kaleb and Rylee should be arriving sometime after nine."

He nodded, and they continued their meal in silence. As the evening wore on, River rose from his seat. "I'm gonna turn in."

Nova wasn't ready for him to leave, but she refrained from voicing any objections as he quietly exited her room. They remained in a fragile space, the unspoken tension hovering between them.

Sitting on the sofa, Nova was caught in the present moment, no longer dwelling on the past. Eleven o'clock arrived, triggering memories of a night that weighed heavily on her conscience.

After a night of shared intimacy and whispered confessions, River had uttered those three powerful words, "I love you." Nova's smile had concealed the turmoil within, but his words had brought a sudden rush of panic. She'd sprung out of bed, fabricating an excuse about her mother needing assistance.

Fifteen minutes later, she'd returned, feigning calmness. River, ever observant, had asked about her mother. She'd assured him everything was fine, inviting him back into their shared embrace. But as they made love again, a shadow of unease had crept over Nova.

In the quiet aftermath, she'd slipped out of bed, tiptoed out of the room with her clothes and left without a trace. The memory now propelled her to River's door. She needed to confront the ghosts of the past to explain why she had vanished that night and left California for Charlotte.

Nova paused in the hallway outside his room to take several calming breaths. She inhaled deeply and exhaled slowly, then knocked on his door, hoping to bridge the gap between the present and the unresolved fragments of their shared history. At least if they discussed it, this would end the tension that was their constant companion.

"Has something happened?" River asked when he opened the door. He looked instantly concerned.

"No," she quickly assured him. "I...I need to talk to you."

His eyebrows rose in surprise. "About what?"

"About *us*."

River shook his head, the dim light casting shadows on

his face. "No… There's nothing to talk about, Nova. Besides, it's late and I'm exhausted."

"I just need to explain myself…"

"Nova, you leaving me like that… It was a cowardly move." His voice was laced with anger. "And after everything we'd been through."

Her heart swelled with pain and fear, her past mistakes coming back to haunt her. She desperately wanted to make things right with him before it was too late.

River's next words rang in her ears: "It's eighteen months too late."

Nova felt dizzy as tears threatened to spill from her eyes. "I…I didn't want to fall in love," she whispered, her voice trembling. "I'd just lost my father… Then I met you. Back then, I wasn't sure if it was a way to avoid dealing with my grief or if it was something more. I was confused, hurting, and just not in the right mental state for a relationship. I came here to say that I'm sorry for hurting you."

Nova turned away, suddenly needing space. She felt the weight of his gaze on her body as she walked away, fighting back the tears in her eyes.

As she went back to her room in silence, Nova tried to steady her breathing and calm the racing of her heart. She knew that River was right—they couldn't change the past. But she couldn't help feeling disappointed.

She lay in bed, feeling an emptiness in her chest where love should have been.

Chapter Nine

River couldn't believe Nova suddenly wanted to have a conversation. There was a time when he would have welcomed a discussion, but it was much too late for that now. It had taken him a long time to get over her. He wasn't about to let her dredge up that pain again.

He had never been the type of person who had scores of women chasing after him. River had always been considered the nerdy type. It didn't bother him to be called a nerd. He wore that label with pride.

Before Nova, there had only been one girl whom he'd dated for four years. While he cared for her, River had never been in love until the day Nova walked into his life. The time they spent together was one of the happiest in his life.

Until he woke up to find her gone without saying goodbye. Without saying anything.

River's pride wouldn't let him contact her once he returned to Charlotte. He spent much of his time chasing criminals. He didn't have any interest in pursuing women. He desired a simple, uncomplicated relationship. He'd dated a couple of women after Nova, but not for long. No one made River feel the way she had. No woman had come close. But that was another time and place.

River decided to call his sister. He didn't want to sit there in his room being pitiful or feeling sorry for himself. He wanted pleasant conversation.

When Bonnie answered, he said, "Hey, sis. I'm calling to check in as promised."

"I'm glad to hear from you. Are you traveling?"

"Yes," he responded.

"Any chance you'll be coming to Sacramento?"

"Not right now," River said. "I'm in the middle of an investigation."

"Oh."

He heard the disappointment in her voice. "You know the plane flies both ways. Why don't you come visit me?"

"I'd love that."

"Send me some dates and I'll fly you to LA. There's this new restaurant in Marina del Rey that I know you'll love."

"I can't wait," Bonnie said. "I need a vacation, too."

She'd spent the past two years taking care of their mother. Now that Mary was gone, Bonnie had returned to the hospital as a nurse.

"I mean it," River said. "Look at your calendar and get back to me. We'll spend some time together after I close this case I'm working on."

"I will," Bonnie responded. "Looking forward to it."

They talked for a few minutes more before hanging up.

The weight of the recent events pressed heavily on River's shoulders. The murder of Mateo, the agency's star witness against the Mancuso cartel, and the disappearance of Mateo's wife had thrown a meticulously built case into chaos. It was a setback that demanded a recalibration of his approach.

River stared at his notes, mapping out the intricate connections he had painstakingly pieced together. The photos of Mateo and his wife seemed to mock him, their faces a haunting reminder of the cost of this relentless pursuit.

His mind raced, searching for a thread to pull, a lead to follow. A flicker of determination sparked as River reached for his phone. Dialing, he waited for the familiar voice on the other end.

"Kenny, it's me. Did you manage to persuade Rico Alfaro to give up his supplier?"

"He claims he's willing to take the fall. My gut tells me he's been in cahoots with the Mancuso cartel."

River released a sigh of frustration. "We need to convince him that we'll go as far as putting the word on the street that he's a snitch."

His partner's agreement resonated through the line, and River hung up, his mind racing with possibilities. He needed to revisit every lead, every contact and every piece of intelligence they had gathered. He couldn't afford to overlook anything, not if he wanted to salvage what remained of the case and bring Johnny Boy to justice for Mateo and the deaths of his friend Jason and another agent.

River and Special Agent Jason Turner's friendship was forged in the face of danger and a shared purpose. They had stood side by side, confronting the ruthless Mancuso cartel, and with each mission they completed together, their bond grew stronger. From the moment they were introduced in the dimly lit corridors of DEA headquarters, there was an instant connection—a recognition that they were cut from the same cloth, driven by an unyielding determination to bring justice to those who sought to spread fear and chaos.

Their friendship went beyond mere camaraderie; they were like brothers, not only because of their shared experiences but also due to a deep mutual respect and trust. Jason had been there for River during his darkest moments, offering unwavering support and encouragement when the weight of their mission threatened to crush him. And River had returned the favor, standing by Jason's side and willing to sacrifice his life to protect his friend from harm.

But then came the day when tragedy struck, shattering their world and leaving River to pick up the pieces. Jason's death at the hands of the Mancuso cartel was a devastating blow, one that left River consumed with grief and anger. The loss of his friend was like an open wound, a constant reminder of the dangers they faced and the ruthless enemies they were fighting against.

In the aftermath of Jason's death, the stakes were higher than ever before. The Mancuso cartel operated without consequence, their power spreading like a disease through society. But River refused to let his friend's sacrifice be in vain. He clung to hope that he would find a thread that would unravel the cartel's empire and bring an end to their reign of terror. For Jason's sake, he would stop at nothing to put an end to the Mancuso cartel's tyranny.

After a shower, River sat in a chair, his legs propped on the ottoman, watching television. His thoughts drifted back to Nova. He wondered what she was doing right now.

River felt terrible for how he'd reacted when she came to his room; it was an unexpected move on Nova's part— one he had never seen coming.

He hadn't changed his mind about sending her away. It had been the right thing to do. River couldn't afford to lose concentration on the job he had to do.

THE FOLLOWING DAY, Nova ate breakfast alone in her room. She hadn't bothered to check in with River because she'd had enough of his attitude. Besides, she didn't want him getting any closer to her. It would only make things more dangerous for them both.

Nova took a deep breath and then a sip of herbal tea. She had a job to do, which required her complete focus.

Shortly after 8:30, the phone in her room rang.

Sighing softly, Nova answered it. "Hello…"

"Good morning. I was checking to see if you're awake," River said.

"Actually, I've been up for a couple of hours. I just finished eating breakfast."

"So did I," he responded. "What time are you expecting Kaleb and his wife?"

"Within the hour. Their plane landed thirty minutes ago."

"I'll come to your room whenever they get here," River said.

Nova didn't reply.

"Did you hear what I said?"

"I heard you," she uttered. "I'll ring your room."

Nova hung up before River could respond.

Deep down, she really didn't have a right to be angry with him. River was entitled to his feelings. Nova wasn't the type of person who carried grudges for years. She chose to either settle them or purge them. Her parents had always told her that life was too short to hold on to bad feelings.

When Kaleb and Rylee arrived, Nova called River. "Hey, they're here."

He was at her door within minutes.

"River, oh man… It's good to see you," Kaleb said when he entered the room. "It's been a long time."

"It sure has," he remarked. "*Kaleb Stone.* I hear you're a married man now."

"Happily married man," he said. "This is my wife, Rylee."

River shook her hand. "It's nice to meet you."

Nova watched River interact with Kaleb. He was smiling, his body more at ease. She wished he were that way around her.

She indicated the small kitchenette. "We can sit over there."

They gathered around the table to discuss the de Leon investigation.

Rylee sat beside her, saying, "Nova, I hope you know how much your father meant to me. I really hate that he lost his life trying to keep me safe."

"My dad died doing what he loved," she responded.

"How is your mother?" Kaleb asked.

Nova smiled. "She's great. Mom keeps busy by volunteering at church and a shelter for homeless women and children."

"Do you have any leads on Mateo's wife?" Rylee asked.

"Not really," Nova answered. "Her parents live in the area, so River and I flew out here to see if she was with them."

Kaleb looked at River. "What's the DEA's part in this?"

"We're hoping that Arya de Leon might have information critical to our investigation. We know Mateo didn't give us everything he had on the Mancuso cartel. I think it was because he was hoping for some type of leverage. He might have been planning to negotiate with Johnny Boy or Poppy for his life, or he was going to try to blackmail them. All this is speculation until we find Arya."

"If what you suspect is true," Kaleb said, "if Mateo gave evidence to his wife for safekeeping...that information could possibly help us dismantle the cartel."

River nodded in agreement. "Exactly." Especially now that their key witness was dead.

Nova knew that Rylee and Kaleb wanted to tear down the cartel just as much as she and River did.

"We're willing to lend our assistance and resources to you both," Rylee said.

Nova smiled. "Thanks."

"I was told by a CI that Manuel DeSoto…Mateo…tried to blackmail Poppy before he disappeared into WITSEC," Rylee said. "He claimed to have copies of deeds and information on all the properties and businesses owned by the cartel. He offered to sell it to her for ten million dollars. He said he'd go away, and they'd never hear from him again."

Nova nodded, familiar with the intel. "Apparently, Poppy didn't believe him," Nova responded. "That was such a stupid move on his part."

Shaking his head, River interjected, "Mateo only narrowly escaped when Johnny Boy discovered he'd been skimming money off the top. If Johnny Boy was the one targeting Mateo's family, Mateo might have sought him out for revenge."

She nodded, though she didn't spare him a glance. She didn't want to give Kaleb and Rylee the impression of tension between them.

"What happens when you find Arya?" Kaleb asked. "Are you putting her back in the program under a new alias?"

"I just need to find her," Nova responded with a slight shrug.

She suddenly felt like she needed some air. She stood up and walked over to the balcony. She opened the sliding glass door and stepped outside.

"Nova, you look troubled," Kaleb said when he joined her on the balcony.

"I keep thinking about Mateo and Arya. I can't help but feel as if I failed them somehow."

"Nova, Mateo's death isn't on you. He took it upon himself to leave WITSEC. He knew the risks, regardless of his reason."

She looked over at Kaleb. "River told me the same thing. But the reality is that Mateo was under my protection. I should've put him under twenty-four-hour security because I knew he was beginning to spiral out of control. I went out to see him, but it was too late."

"You didn't do anything wrong. At the time, he wasn't under a high-threat situation, Nova. There wasn't a need for additional security. Look, I know all too well how it feels to lose a witness. It's not a good feeling," Kaleb said. "I don't know if your dad ever told you, but that's why I left the Marshals."

She studied him. "He didn't."

"My witness left the program just like Mateo," he said. "It's what got him killed, but I took his death personally. I didn't want to lose another one, even if it was caused by their own actions."

"I'm beginning to feel the same way. After we find Arya, I'm not sure I'll stay with the agency. I joined the Marshals because I wanted to work with my dad…" Nova paused momentarily, saying, "I'm not going to lose Arya."

"We'll do everything possible to help you find her."

"Kaleb, I'm so glad you're here."

"Me, too." He placed an arm around her. "I want you to know that Easton would be so proud of you. I bet he's looking down at you with a big grin."

She glanced up at him. "I hope so. How is Nate?" Nova asked.

"My brother is doing well. I've been trying to convince him to leave Wisconsin and join me in Los Angeles. He's not trying to hear it."

She laughed. "How do *you* like living in California?"

"It's fine. I'm happy anywhere Rylee is," Kaleb responded.

"Kaleb, that's a nice thing to say," Nova responded, masking the pain in her voice. "I can see how genuinely happy you are with Rylee." She couldn't help but think of her short time with River and how it had left a lasting imprint on her heart. Despite trying to move on, memories of their time together haunted her.

"I'm surprised some man hasn't snatched you up yet."

"One-track mind," Nova stated. "I've been focused on my career. Besides, the badge intimidates some of the men I've dated. I'll probably end up with someone in law enforcement. They seem to be the only people who understand me."

Kaleb smiled. "I used to feel that way, too."

"And you ended up marrying someone in the field."

"That wasn't the deciding factor, though," he responded. "I would've married Rylee no matter what."

"That's great. Maybe one day I'll get lucky enough to find my Mr. Right. I'm not really in any hurry, though."

"You just have to be open to loving and being loved, Nova."

She smiled. "I hear you."

Nova really wanted to share her life with someone special. It was just that she hadn't met him yet. Well…she'd blown it with the man who'd come close. He would always hold a special place in her heart. She definitely had regrets. Nova wished now that she'd handled things differently.

Her chance with River had come and gone. No point in dwelling on the past. Life was meant to be lived looking ahead and not in the rearview mirror.

RIVER EYED NOVA's interaction with Kaleb from across the room and wondered what they could be discussing. He'd never seen her like this. From the moment he'd met her, River had quickly learned that Nova was always sure of herself and liked to be in control. The woman outside with Kaleb seemed reflective and doubtful. He wondered what could have made her so upset.

"How long have you known Nova?" Rylee asked, cutting into his musings.

"A couple of years," River answered, trying to sound nonchalant. "We worked on a case together. I hadn't talked to her since. Until now."

"I see. Nova's father was my handler when I was in WITSEC," Rylee said. "My relationship with her actually developed after Kaleb and I got married."

She leaned down to open her laptop. "Have you conducted a property search?"

"I checked for listings under Mateo's and Arya's names. Nothing came up."

Rylee sat down at the table. "I'll run her parents' names and those of other known relatives. Maybe we'll get a hit. Arya could be hiding in one of the family properties."

Nova approached, trailed by Kaleb, and said, "I took some photographs from the Lozano house. Maybe we can find out where they were taken. There's nothing but dates written on the back of the pictures."

"I'll scan them and send them to the tech at HSI," Rylee said.

"It's worth a try," Nova agreed as she laid them on the table. "River and I have already conducted a property search. We have a list of places to check out. One of which is a house given to Ramona Lozano by her brother before he died," Nova said. "It's in Oceanside. I need to change out of these sweatpants. Then I'll be ready to leave."

River thought she looked nice in the tank top and navy sweats but decided to keep his opinion to himself.

"Kaleb, you can join me in my room while Nova gets dressed," River said. "I need to grab something before we go.

"I had no idea that you were with Homeland Security," River said as he and Kaleb walked across the hall to his room. "I thought you were done with this life."

"I thought so, too," he responded. "My brother and I were partners in a private security firm. I sold my shares to him after Rylee and I got married."

"Did you join HSI because of your wife?" River inquired.

"Partly. While I was trying to keep Rylee safe, it made me realize just how much I missed being part of the action."

"How long have you been working the Mancuso cartel investigation?" Kaleb asked.

"Not long. I inherited the case from another agent who left the job. I think it was given to me because of my recent investigation into the Torres cartel. But I have personal reasons for wanting this case—a close friend of mine was murdered at the hands of Johnny Boy."

"The Torres cartel… That was *you*?" Kaleb asked. "That was a huge bust. Great job, River."

"It was a team effort coordinated with HSI, ATF and LAPD."

"Still, it was good work. Man, don't sell yourself short."

"Thanks," River replied.

He wanted to ask about Nova but decided against it. Kaleb wasn't aware of their past and River thought it best not to bring up the subject. *Keep the focus on the job.*

Chapter Ten

"Kaleb looks happier than I've ever seen him," Nova said. She'd freshened up and was back in the kitchenette with Rylee. "I have to say that you two are so good for each other."

Rylee smiled. "I've never loved anyone as much as I love him."

"Did you fall in love with him while he protected you?"

"The first thing I noticed about Kaleb was those piercing gray eyes. We were initially attracted to one another, but at the time, our main focus was keeping me alive and out of the cartel's reach."

"I love a happy ending," Nova said.

"You sound like a romantic."

"Not at all," she responded. "When things get serious... I run." To be honest, there was only one man she'd run from. It was hard to put into words what was going on in her head back then. She'd just lost her father and felt like she couldn't catch her breath.

"Have you ever tried to figure out why?" Rylee asked.

"I don't know."

"Sounds like you panic."

Nova nodded. "The excitement of this intense connection clashed with the heaviness of my sorrow and left me feeling lost, like I was spiraling out of control. I didn't know which way was up, and every emotion seemed to blur together into a confusing mess. In the middle of all that chaos, it hit me—I hadn't really taken the time to grieve for my dad properly. His loss was this gaping hole in my heart, and instead of facing it, I let myself get swept away by the whirlwind romance. I was scared, Rylee, scared that I was losing myself in the middle of it all. I really messed things up between us and I don't know how to fix it."

"What happened?"

"I made the toughest decision I've ever had to make—I ran away. No words…no note…nothing."

"No…" Rylee offered a sympathetic look.

"Yeah, and I regret the way I left," Nova admitted, a wave of sadness flowing through her. "I should've stayed there and talked to him. I should've told him what I was feeling at the time."

"How long has it been?"

"Eighteen months."

"Do you still see him, or can you get in contact with him?" Rylee inquired.

"I've run into him recently," Nova said.

"I'm assuming it didn't go very well."

"There's a lot of tension between us." She turned to check her reflection in the mirror before saying, "I guess we'd better get going."

Rylee nodded, standing up. "Nova, I have a feeling everything will work out between you and River."

Turning to face Rylee, she asked, "How did you know I was talking about River?"

"Girl, you can cut the tension between you two with a knife."

"Really?"

"Yes." Rylee grinned. "But things will get better between you."

Nova picked up her black tote. As they walked to the front door, she said, "Rylee, I really hope you're right about me and River. I miss his friendship."

"Is that all?"

"No, but it's all I can expect from him now, and even that's asking a lot."

River and Kaleb were in the hallway waiting.

Nova met River's gaze; then she looked away almost immediately. He was such a handsome man. Her eyes traveled down to the white polo shirt and jeans he wore.

Ten minutes later, they were walking through the parking deck to the SUV.

They made the forty-five-minute drive to Oceanside.

While Nova sat in the back seat chatting with Rylee, Kaleb and River talked about how they met and the case that brought them together.

Nova watched the passing streets and immediately fell in love with the area's laid-back vibe. She especially liked the quaint little homes. Nestled in the coastal town was the military base Camp Pendleton. Her father had once been stationed there when he was in the Marines. Nova had been too young then to remember anything now about the base or the area.

The Lozano house wasn't too far from the Oceanside Pier. The exterior was painted in soothing shades of seafoam and aqua. From where they were parked, they could see the patio featured a firepit, lounge furniture and a grill. Nova imagined it was the perfect spot for evenings with family and friends to sit back and chill, watching picturesque sunsets, toasting marshmallows or making s'mores.

Her attention shifted to the house as they sat in the car across from the corner property, watching as a middle-aged woman walked out to retrieve the rest of the bags from the trunk of a car.

"Somebody's home. Possibly the housekeeper," Nova suggested.

River removed his sunglasses. "Judging from the groceries...Pablo Lozano and his wife must be here, too, and they're planning to stay a while."

Nova released the breath she'd been holding. "I think it's best I speak to the parents alone," she said. "River, you might intimidate them."

"Why don't I go with you?" Rylee suggested. "Two women won't seem so threatening."

Kaleb nodded in agreement.

She exited the car, and she and Rylee walked to the door. Rylee rang the bell. "Here goes..."

"Hello," Nova said when the woman they'd seen earlier opened the door.

She and Rylee showed their badges and introduced themselves before Nova added, "We're looking for Mr. and Mrs. Lozano."

"They're not here," the housekeeper responded. "They left yesterday. They're traveling, and I don't know when they'll return."

"Do you happen to know where they went?" Nova inquired, wondering about the groceries.

The woman shook her head. "No, they didn't tell me anything. Just that they would be out of town for a few weeks. Mrs. Lozano said it was a much-needed vacation." She smiled gently before adding, "They haven't traveled much since they lost their daughter."

Rylee nodded. "Do they always leave without telling you where they're going?" she asked.

"They tell me only what they want me to know."

"Someone broke into the house in San Diego," Rylee stated. "Whoever it was killed the housekeeper."

The woman gasped. "Yolanda…"

"Yes," Nova confirmed. "We noticed the bags of groceries you brought into the house. It's a lot for a house no one currently lives in."

She looked from Rylee to Nova. "What do y'all want with Mr. and Mrs. Lozano? These are good people."

"Here is my card," Nova said. "I just want to make sure they're safe."

"Wait here…"

The housekeeper left for a moment before returning with a photo in hand. "I'm not sure where it is, but I think it might be in North Carolina. The Lozano family used to go there every summer. It belongs to one of Mrs. Lozano's cousins."

Nova's face lit up with a smile. "Thank you." The photo was different from the ones they'd found.

The photograph showed a beautiful, large lakefront home with white exteriors and a charming stone pathway leading up to the front door. The house was surrounded by lush green trees and a sprawling lawn that faded into the crystal blue lake in the background. There was a glimpse of a wooden dock extending from the backyard toward the water, lined with cozy lounge chairs and a small boat tied to its side. The clear blue sky and fluffy white clouds above completed the picturesque scene.

She climbed back into the car, unsure if they were getting closer or falling behind in their investigation.

RIVER PEERED AT NOVA, who sat in the back seat with Rylee. He'd been trying not to stare all morning. He yearned to unpin her hair, allowing it to flow free around her face, but quickly forced the image out of his mind. The only thing between them now was their missing witness and her parents.

"I emailed a copy of that new photograph to one of the techs at HSI," Rylee told the group. "Hopefully, they'll be able to narrow down the location for us."

Nova looked up at River, saying, "The housekeeper thinks Arya's parents are in North Carolina."

"Where?"

"She didn't know for sure, but we're thinking this is where this picture may have been taken."

River said, "That's great if it's in North Carolina, but it's a long shot. That backdrop could be anywhere."

"If it were just the beach, I might agree with you," Nova stated as she studied the photograph. "But look at those mountains… This house sits on a lake."

While waiting for the light to turn green, she handed the picture to River.

"I think you might be right," he said after returning it to her. He tried not to focus too much on the feeling of his fingers brushing hers as he'd passed the picture back. "Now we need some luck to find the exact location."

"Sounds so simple, doesn't it?" Nova smiled.

"Hopefully, my tech person will call back with some good news," Rylee said.

The traffic light switched to green, and they continued down the road, the anticipation palpable in the air. The journey to uncover Arya's parents' whereabouts had become a puzzle, and each piece could lead them closer to the missing woman.

As the car rolled forward, Nova couldn't shake the sense of urgency that propelled them back to the East Coast, chasing elusive answers against North Carolina's landscape.

When they returned to the hotel, Rylee said, "I've been charged with putting together a multiagency task force. My team will be in this area for a meeting with the San Diego police and I asked them to stop by. They should be arriving within the hour."

"That's great," Nova said. "I'm looking forward to meeting them." She sat down and opened up her laptop. "While we're waiting for an address on that property, I'm going to go back through the phone records of Arya's parents. I want to see which relatives they have been in contact with. It looks like they may be trying to cover their tracks."

"It will help keep them alive," Kaleb said.

"But for how long?" River responded.

That was Nova's concern as well. Her heart raced as she realized the gravity of Johnny Boy's actions. The men he sent were ruthless and calculating, experts in hunting down their targets. She knew they would stop at nothing to find their intended victims, leaving a trail of destruction in their wake.

Fifty minutes later, there was a knock on the door.

"They're here," Rylee announced.

As Rylee introduced each team member, Nova took a moment to observe them individually.

Sabra Gomez stood with an air of authority, her dark hair pulled back in a tight bun and dressed professionally in a white button-up shirt and black blazer. Next to her was Tauren Gray, whose mixed heritage could be seen in his rich cream-colored skin and serious expression. He mentioned that he and River had trained together at the DEA Academy in Quantico.

Maisie Wells, on loan from LAPD, exuded confidence with her twist-out hairstyle and regal posture. Rolle Livingston from ATF had a neat ponytail that showed off his defined features, and FBI agent Harper Arness's short hair gave off a professional vibe.

Finally, there was HSI agent Seth Majors, who commanded attention with his tall stature and commanding presence, framed by clean-shaven dark brown skin and closely cropped black hair.

"Wow," Nova murmured. "Looks like you've put together quite a team."

"I wanted you all to meet because we share a common interest," Rylee stated. "We're currently focused on the Mancuso cartel."

"We heard the DEA lost a witness recently," Tauren said.

Nodding, River responded, "He was mine."

When everyone was seated, Nova said, "I was his case agent in witness protection, and now his wife is missing. We think she's gone into hiding. She's in danger."

"There's been some chatter about a missing package," Sabra said. "Maybe this is what they've been talking about. But something else is going on that they seem to consider more urgent. We've decoded some of the conversations originating in Mexico and discovered that the cartel has several tractor trailers leaving the Arizona/Mexico border. They're said to be carrying *lettuce*. In this instance, lettuce refers to cocaine. Several hundred kilos."

Nova knew that the codes and lingo used by drug traffickers were only limited by the imagination. Kilos had often been referred to as batteries, oranges, melons...

"Johnny Boy has been on a pretty good run," Rylee stated. "It's time we stop him."

"How does this man manage to keep eluding arrests?" Harper asked. "Even Calderon was apprehended eventually."

"Because he's smarter than Calderon ever was." Nova's

jaw clenched as she replied, her eyes burning with determination. "Johnny Boy knows how to stay under the radar, never getting too comfortable or predictable." She couldn't help but secretly hope that he would slip up, a glimmer of desperation creeping into her tone. They needed a break from this endless game of cat and mouse.

Rolle interjected, "We all know he has a pretty good system going. His life is like a shell game. Johnny Boy has several body doubles, just like Raul Mancuso did. Ninety percent of the time, no one knows where he or the doubles are. The difference between Raul and Johnny Boy is that he didn't hire these look-alikes to fool the Mexican and US governments—they're in place to fool the people closest to him."

Nova said, "According to Manuel DeSoto, outside of Poppy, only a few people can speak to Johnny Boy in person—and the families of those with that privilege live in luxury at Johnny Boy's expense. It's how he rewards their loyalty."

"Naw…it's not a reward. That's all about power," Rolle stated. "Johnny Boy wants the people around him to know that not only are their lives in his hands, but their family's lives are, too."

River nodded in agreement. "My witness told the DEA that Johnny Boy had one of his lieutenants killed because the man brought a personal phone to a dinner hosted by him. He's always been paranoid about anything that might be a tracking device, a recorder or a camera. The only known picture of Johnny Boy was taken when he was nineteen and booked for a murder in Jamaica. He sat in jail for about a week. During that time, all the witnesses to that murder ended up dead, so he was released. They couldn't go forward without a witness, and his alibi was solid. Johnny Boy disappeared after that."

"How do we know that the man arrested in Jamaica wasn't one of Johnny Boy's doubles?" Harper asked. "Maybe the real Johnny Boy murdered the witnesses. Think about it… His fingerprints disappeared… If it wasn't for my witness, we wouldn't have what information we have now. Johnny Boy is still pretty much a shadow."

"I have a man in custody right now…Rico Alfaro…but he's not saying a word," River announced. "He fears Johnny Boy more than doing life in prison."

"He can't elude us forever," Rylee stated. "We will dismantle his routes truck by truck—come down hard on his people until someone is willing to talk."

"What will y'all do with this new information you've decoded?" River asked.

Nova wondered the same thing, but he'd beat her to it.

"The team is heading to Arizona this afternoon. They'll connect with local ATF and DEA agents to assist with intercepting the trucks," Rylee responded. "We just scored a win when we seized fifty pounds of cocaine in a shipment of what was supposed to be packs of coconut flour a few days ago, and we're hoping for another."

"Johnny Boy might be in Arizona then," River said. "I heard he likes to be nearby if there's a problem. He wants to know the person responsible for any mistakes."

"If this is true, then he isn't focused on Arya," Nova responded.

River eyed her. "That's because he's got people out there searching for her. Trust me…he's not letting up."

Seth checked his watch. "We need to pick up Max."

"Who is Max?" she asked.

"Oh yes, we have another team member," Rylee announced. "Max. He is Seth's K-9 partner."

"What kind of dog?" Nova wanted to know.

"He's a Belgian Malinois," Seth answered. "He's six years old and the best partner I've ever had. Max is a dual-purpose dog trained for patrol and narcotics."

"Where's Max now?" she asked.

"He's getting some much-needed grooming," Seth stated. "My sister owns a shop down here, so we dropped Max off before coming here."

After a few more minutes of discussion, Rylee's team left the hotel.

"I wanted you all to meet because I hope that we'll continue to work together in this war against the drug cartels," Rylee stated.

"What did you have in mind when you mentioned working together?" Nova asked.

"I meant that I'd like for you and River to join the team. Nova, you'd have to relocate to Los Angeles. I'll understand if this is not something you're interested in doing right now."

She glanced over at River. He seemed as surprised as she was by Rylee's offer. Nova didn't know what he would decide, but she knew what she would do—she wanted a change. Relocating wasn't a problem because Nova loved the West Coast and could see herself living here full-time.

It would also place her and River in the same city. She didn't know how he would feel about it, but it didn't matter because this was about her career. She wouldn't let their past get in the way of her aspirations.

Chapter Eleven

River's eyebrows rose in surprise over Rylee's job offer.

He was even more shocked when Nova said, "I'd be interested in joining. I've been trying to figure out my next move after Arya is safe, and I really believe this is it."

Rylee smiled. "That's great. We can talk about this in detail after we find Arya."

River sat quietly, observing the women as they talked. He was stunned by the idea of Nova moving to Los Angeles. While the task force sounded interesting and like a great opportunity, he loved his job and wasn't looking for a change. He wasn't opposed to helping if needed, but he was finally up for a promotion he'd been wanting—now wasn't the time to leave.

He personally didn't think it was a good idea for Nova to relocate to Los Angeles. It was too close for his comfort. It was a big enough city to keep them from running into one another. However, because they were both in law enforcement, he and Nova were bound to move within the same circles.

I can't make Nova's career moves about me. No point in worrying about something that might not happen.

The sound of her laughter was like a siren's call, luring him back to the warmth and comfort of their past love. But as he watched Nova laughing with Kaleb, River couldn't help but feel a twinge of fear in his heart. A fear that if he let her back into his life, she would once again leave him broken and alone. The familiar excitement at the sound of her laugh quickly dissipated as he remembered the pain and heartache she had caused before. He knew deep down that letting her back in meant risking his heart all over again, and he wasn't sure if he could survive another shattering blow.

He couldn't deny that Nova still had an effect on him, although he'd never admit this truth aloud to anyone. River struggled with admitting it to himself.

Nova walked over to where he was sitting. "What did you think of Rylee's team?"

"I've known Tauren a long time, but the others... They were cool," he responded.

She nodded. "I thought they were an impressive group of people."

Nova didn't spare him so much as a glance when she walked past, crossing the room to where Rylee was sitting. They were looking at something on the laptop computer.

River got up to make a phone call. He strode to the door, opened it and walked across the hall. The case he was calling about was in his room. Although his focus was on finding Arya, he still continued investigating the other assigned cases.

He had to return to Nova's room afterward. They were going to discuss the next course of action to find the Lozanos and Arya. He also placed a call to local police to send someone to check out one other house in San Diego that belonged to Arya's grandparents. It was currently listed for sale.

When River returned to Nova's room, he was met by her frosty stare. Working in a tense environment wasn't good for either of them. If they weren't careful, this tension between them could turn into something more toxic.

River didn't want that, and he was sure Nova didn't either.

"HEY, NOVA... I don't want to get into your business, but are things cool between you and River?" Kaleb inquired while they were sitting in chairs on the balcony. They had taken a short break.

Nova had come out to watch the sun go down. She wanted to experience a California sunset.

"Why do you ask that?" She wondered if Rylee had mentioned their earlier conversation to him.

"I noticed that you two don't seem to have much to say to one another outside of your investigation. Things between you seem kinda strained."

"Rylee mentioned the same thing earlier," Nova stated. "You might as well know what happened... Eighteen months ago, River and I worked on a case together. We spent two wonderful weeks together. Things between us started happening so fast that I could barely breathe and panicked. Kaleb...he made me feel things I'd never felt before. I didn't know what to do, so I left without saying anything to him."

"And now?"

"As you can see...he's not exactly fond of me." Her heart ached at the very thought, but she wasn't going to let it show.

"You know that River's responding out of hurt, Nova. If he really didn't want anything to do with you, I doubt he'd be here."

"That's the irony. I was actually trying to save him from heartache, but maybe he needs more time to erase the pain."

"Have you tried to talk to River about what happened?" he asked.

Nova shook her head as terrible regrets assailed her. "He's done a really great job of discouraging any personal conversation. You know Dad used to be the one who gave me relationship advice. I wish I could talk to him about this."

Kaleb embraced her. "I'm sorry Easton's not here, but you can always come to me, Nova. I'll do the best I can. Your dad was my go-to person for relationship advice as well."

"I feel like I've failed him in some way," she said. "He never lost a witness. I knew Mateo and Arya were headstrong. I should have…"

"Don't torture yourself like this. It doesn't do you any good."

Water welled up in her eyes and overflowed, rolling down her cheeks.

Nova pulled a tissue out of her pocket and wiped away her tears. She clenched her jaw to kill the sob in her throat. "I don't know why I'm getting so emotional."

"Our jobs are stressful, and you're still grieving. Sometimes, we all need to sit down and have a good cry."

With a deep breath, she forced herself to head back to work, trying to impose an iron control on her emotions.

Kaleb excused himself and went inside to speak with his wife.

"Are you okay?" River asked when she walked back inside. "You looked like you were crying."

Nova was surprised by his question. "I'm good. I just had an emotional moment over my dad."

"I know you must miss him very much. Are you up to discuss a plan of action? If not, we can do it later."

"No…of course. We can do it now."

Nova grabbed a water bottle and a snack bag of peanuts from a basket in the kitchenette, taking them to the table.

Rylee stepped away from them when her phone rang.

"We found it," she said after hanging up. "The house in the photo is in the Lake Glenville area. Another relative."

"Arya never once mentioned that she had family in North Carolina," Nova stated. "We never would've been placed there. She intentionally withheld that information. I know that she and Mateo vacationed there for the past two years." Shaking her head, she uttered, "Those two..."

River looked up from his file.

"That's probably where Arya's been all this time," she said. "She may have felt it was the safest place to go."

He agreed. "Lake Glenville is about three and a half hours from Charlotte."

"We should book seats on the next flight to Atlanta," River said. "It's two and a half hours from Lake Glenville."

Nova agreed.

Kaleb and Rylee prepared to head back to the airport.

"It was so good seeing you and Kaleb," Nova said. "Thanks for everything."

Rylee stood with her hand on the doorknob. "I'll be in touch within the next week or so regarding the task force."

"Great! Because I'm really looking forward to hearing more about it," Nova responded. "I'm ready for something new."

"We're booked on a flight leaving tonight at seven," River announced.

Rylee said, "Kaleb and I want to take you to dinner before you head to the airport."

"Fine by me," Nova responded with a smile.

She glanced over at River, who said, "Sure."

Nova quickly packed her suitcase because they were heading to the airport right after they finished eating. River went back to his own room to do the same.

After checking out and putting the luggage in the SUV, they decided to eat at the restaurant in the hotel.

"This is a nice place," Rylee said.

Nova glanced around. "Yes, it is…"

She was saddened by Kaleb and Rylee's leaving. They were the perfect buffer between her and River. She wasn't looking forward to being alone with him again.

"I GUESS THIS wasn't a completely wasted trip," River stated shortly after the plane took off. "Unfortunately, Yolanda was an innocent victim in all this."

Nova agreed. "We probably wouldn't have found out about the house in North Carolina otherwise."

"I hate to put a negative spin on this, but there's a chance that Arya or her parents might not be at this house either."

"I know, River," she said. "But we'll cross that bridge when we get to it." Nova felt the tension rising between them like a thick fog, suffocating and uncomfortable. They were being very careful to keep space from each other even though they were seated beside one another.

"So, you're thinking about leaving the Marshals?" River asked, his voice laced with skepticism.

Nova gave him an icy stare. "I've given it serious thought… What about you?"

His response was a dismissive shake of his head. "Not interested. I'm happy where I am."

She clenched her jaw, struggling to keep her emotions in check. They needed to talk about what had happened in their past, no matter how painful it may be. But last time she'd tried, it hadn't gone well.

Nova sighed, feeling frustrated and unheard. "I just hate all this tension between us," she finally said, her voice low and strained.

River's expression softened slightly. "I didn't mean for things to turn out this way. I don't think I've been rude to you."

"You haven't exactly been warm and fuzzy either," Nova retorted, her tone sharp with hurt.

"I never meant to hurt you," River answered, his words genuine but guarded. "I just don't want things to get out of hand."

Nova's heart sank at his admission. So, he didn't trust himself around her. She couldn't blame him after what had happened between them.

"Just so we're clear," she said, keeping her gaze fixed ahead. "I am capable of keeping my distance and staying professional."

"I know that."

The comment ended things on a bittersweet note, both silently agreeing to put aside their issues for the sake of the investigation. But as River pulled out a bag of potato chips and offered some to her, Nova couldn't help but feel a sense of unease and sadness linger between them. Would they ever be able to repair their fractured relationship fully?

Only time would tell. She shook her head at his offer of a snack.

"You sure you don't want any?" River asked. "Because I've seen you staring them down. I'm pretty sure I heard your stomach growling, too."

Nova knew he was trying to lighten the mood. She decided to accept his peace offering. "It was probably your stomach you heard. Considering you only ordered a salad at dinner," she teased.

"C'mon… It's been a while since we shared a bag of potato chips."

"It's been a minute," she responded while settling back in her seat, her unease slowly dissipating.

Nova eyed the bag of chips again, then reached inside.

"I knew you couldn't resist." River smiled.

Giving him a mock roll of her eyes, she took the bag out of his hand.

"I can't believe that you're really thinking about leaving the Queen City," he stated. "When we met, you talked about how much you loved Charlotte."

She nodded. "I do love it there, but I want a more productive role in helping to take down the Mancuso cartel. They're responsible for my father's death. I want to make sure he didn't die in vain."

His eyes widened in surprise. "You never told me that. I don't think you ever mentioned how he died."

"I didn't want to focus on the tragedies in my life back then," Nova responded. "My dad and I... We were close. Losing him is harder than I ever imagined it would be. I feel like there's a hole in my heart."

"I understand," he responded. "I felt that way when I lost my grandmother."

"I have his text messages saved. I read them when I need to talk to him."

He smiled. "I think about all the conversations I used to have with my grandmother. There are times when I can almost hear her voice."

As they talked about the people they'd lost, Nova sank deeper into her seat while trying to stifle a yawn.

"Why don't you try and get a nap in?" River suggested. "We will hit the ground running as soon as we land."

"I really hope we find them this time," she murmured.

"We haven't lost yet."

"We haven't exactly gotten anywhere either." She paused

a moment, then said, "River, don't mind me. You know I'm not a pessimist. This whole thing with Mateo and Arya..." Nova gave herself a mental shake. "You know what... I'm good."

"I know you're frustrated," River said. "I am, too. It's an unspoken part of our job description."

She gave a short chuckle as she stuck a pair of AirPods in her ears and selected a playlist to enjoy. She resolved to let the music revitalize her spirit. When the plane landed, they had to move quickly. They couldn't afford to waste any time heading to Lake Glenville. She hoped fervently that Pablo and Ramona Lozano would be at the house along with Arya.

RIVER TOOK WHAT he considered a power nap during the final hour of the flight. Turned out it was what he needed, because he felt rejuvenated by the time the plane landed in Atlanta.

They rented a car and drove to Lake Glenville, the coastal town located eight miles from Cashiers, NC, in a mountain rainforest.

"It's beautiful up here," Nova said, looking out the passenger-side window.

"It looks like the perfect place to visit if you're a lover of the outdoors," River remarked. He wasn't, so while the landscape was indeed a beauty, it wasn't his thing.

Nova took a sip of her water. "I remember you saying that you weren't the camping or fishing type."

"I'm not. I love the beach, but I've never cared much for the mountains."

She chuckled. "I'm not either. I'll take the beach any day. I did read that there are three waterfalls here."

They made a left turn into a quaint neighborhood. Following the directions of the GPS, River turned right on the first street they approached.

"This is the house that was in the photograph." Nova's voice was a velvet murmur as River slowly passed the home. "It's the one with the dark blue shutters."

River felt his heart race and swallowed hard. "Yes, that's it."

They parked down the street.

"I'm thinking we watch the house for a bit instead of just rushing up to the door," River said. "If they're in there, we don't want to spook them."

"After what they've been through, don't you think seeing a strange car in the neighborhood with two people sitting in it might spook them more?" Nova responded. "I think it's better for us to get out and talk to them."

Shrugging, River said, "Okay. We'll try it your way. Do you think we should wear our vests?"

"Not this time."

They got out of the car and made their way up to the house.

Nova rang the doorbell a few minutes later. She released a soft sigh of relief when the door opened a sliver and Ramona Lozano peered through the crack.

Looking from River to Nova, she asked, "May I help you?"

"Mrs. Lozano, I'm Deputy Marshal Nova Bennett. Your daughter may have mentioned me." She held up her badge. "Is your husband home with you?"

The thin woman looked as if she were about to faint. She ran trembling fingers through her short hair. "Yes, he is. Is he in some kind of trouble?"

"No, he isn't."

Her brow furrowed. "Then why are you looking for him?"

Nova glanced over at River, then back at Ramona. "You know I'm not here about Pablo. I've been searching for the two of you and your daughter. You all could be in danger." She identified Arya by the name she was given at birth.

Nervous, Ramona glanced away. "I'm afraid I don't know where she is. I—"

"Look, I know she's been in contact with you, Mrs. Lozano," Nova interjected. "I'm sure you've heard by now that Yolanda was murdered in your home. The people after you are not playing games. You're all in grave danger, and I'm here to help."

The woman released a shaky breath. "Ava called to warn us that we were in danger, but I haven't heard from her since then, and I don't know where she is."

"Mrs. Lozano, I only want to keep your daughter safe."

Clutching her necklace as if it were a lifeline, Ramona responded, "If I hear from her, I'll let you know if you leave your number with me. All I want is for Ava to come home to us. We miss her terribly. I don't know what that dreadful husband of hers has gotten her into..."

"I want you to know that I'll do everything in my power to keep Arya safe," Nova reassured her. "But I need to find her first."

Ramona gestured for them to enter. "You can search the house, but she's not here." River accepted her invitation to verify that they were alone in the home while Nova sat down in the living room with Ramona.

"Ava said she couldn't tell us where she was—only that we had to leave California," Ramona explained. "We heard about Mateo's family, and then Mateo... Her father and I did as she asked. We left our home and came here." Clutching the gold cross around her neck, Ramona sighed. "Poor Yolanda. I told her that she should visit her family in Mexico. But she wanted to help. We knew someone might be watching the house, and we didn't want anyone to know we'd left. She thought she'd be safe."

"They were either looking for you and your husband… or trying to find your daughter. Don't you see that *we* can protect all of you?" Nova paused momentarily, then added, "If you do hear from her, tell Arya I found her message and I'm on her side."

"I will," Ramona responded. "Thank you."

"My daughter told us to leave and go where nobody would find us," Pablo said when he and River joined them in the living room. "We figured we'd be safe here."

"It wasn't easy locating you," Nova stated. "I must confess that I took some of your photos, and they led us here. Are you sure you can't give us a clue as to where we should look for your daughter?"

"I can't help you," Ramona said, averting her gaze. "I'm sorry."

Nova understood the fear and desperation that gripped the Lozano family. She respected Ramona's decision to keep quiet, even though it made their task more challenging. Her heart went out to them, but without more concrete information, finding Arya would be like searching for a needle in a haystack.

Chapter Twelve

They walked back to the car and got inside.

"It's obvious that Ramona Lozano isn't going to tell us anything because she wants to protect her daughter," Nova said. She was frustrated and needed to vent. "I thought telling them about Yolanda's murder might scare her into telling us where to find Arya, but she's sticking to her story."

"You don't seem convinced," River said.

"I'm not sure what to believe," she responded. "Arya was worried enough to warn them to leave their home... Surely, she'd check in. She'd want to know that they're safe. At least, that's what I would do."

He nodded. "I agree. So, what do you want to do?"

"We should hang around and see if they suddenly have visitors."

They sat there for the next couple of hours.

"There hasn't been any movement coming or going," River said. "There's a café two blocks from the neighborhood. Why don't we pick up something to eat?"

Nodding, Nova said, "Works for me."

They made the trip in silence and River pulled back into the neighborhood. "What's weighing so heavily on your mind?" River asked as they returned to their surveillance spot and started to eat in the car. "You look like you're trying to figure something out. I can almost hear your brain working."

"I was thinking about Mateo," Nova explained. "I think he wanted money to disappear, and this was the only way he thought he'd be able to get it. Unfortunately, now Arya has a target on her back."

"From what I know of Johnny Boy, he'd eliminate Mateo's wife and her entire family to play it safe."

"My gut tells me that Ramona knows where Arya's hiding," Nova said, pulling her hair into a ponytail. "I wish I could get her to trust me."

Glancing around, River said, "Everything seems normal around here. No perceived threats in the area—that's a good thing."

"It is, but I'd feel better if we just sit for a while longer to see if anything happens."

"I don't have a problem with that," he said with a slight shrug.

Nova swallowed hard. She was quickly becoming tired of the runaround. She didn't mind the chase if she were getting results. Right now, she didn't see anything but disappointment. They needed to find Arya, and soon.

RIVER AND NOVA continued to watch the house after dark, but nothing seemed amiss.

Nova pulled out a small bottle and spritzed some of the liquid on her neck.

"Arya's endgame is to be reunited with her parents," he said while trying to ignore the tantalizing scent of her fragrance. She'd opened a window and her scent now wafted to him. "We just have to figure out how they're going to make that happen."

Nova craned her neck and stared at the house. "I really

thought they'd pack a suitcase and take off as soon as we left. Maybe Ramona was telling the truth. Maybe she doesn't know where Arya's hiding."

"The day's not over yet." A few more minutes passed in silence and he tried to think of a conversation starter while they were sitting there in the vehicle. There were so many things River wanted to say to her, and much he didn't want to say. His emotions were conflicted since Nova had come back into his life. It brought back memories of Mary and the way she'd rejected him. The trauma of that experience shaped the man River had become, especially when it came to love.

Nova would never know how hard it was for River to be vulnerable enough to share what he was feeling with her. She'd made him feel safe and then she destroyed that safety. After their relationship ended, River had vowed to never show such vulnerability to anyone ever again. He viewed love as a weakness—one that could be easily exploited.

He chided himself for going down that path. They were on assignment, and making sure the witness and her parents remained unharmed was the priority. Right now, nothing else mattered.

River eyed the license plate of a black truck that passed them.

Nothing was remarkable about it, but it held his attention for the moment. He watched to see if the vehicle slowed as it neared the Lozanos' house.

It kept moving without slowing down.

"Something wrong?" Nova asked.

"No. Just checking out the truck that just passed by. It wasn't anything."

The tags were local. River kept looking to see if it passed by again, but it didn't. Nothing to send off any red flags, but his experienced senses were on alert.

NOVA STRUGGLED TO maintain a professional front, but keeping her mind off the handsome River was a challenge. She wondered how he could be both sexy and frustrating simultaneously. Those kissable lips of his reminded Nova of their time together in the past. Memories that she didn't want to dredge up. Memories she regarded as precious.

They were only precious to her, Nova realized.

The garage door to the Lozano house went up, cutting into her thoughts.

She glanced at the clock. It was one o'clock in the morning.

Pablo walked briskly, carrying a travel bag to the SUV. Ramona followed behind.

Nova nudged River, who'd seen it, too.

"Looks like Arya's parents are about to leave."

"Let's find out where they're going," River said as he started the vehicle.

Nova nodded. "Pull in front of the driveway so they can't leave."

The black truck that cut them off came out of nowhere. River made an abrupt stop to avoid a collision. Nova's body was pushed back and then thrown forward. Her instincts immediately sounded the alarm in her mind. Trouble loomed on the horizon.

"That's the same black truck that passed earlier." River's voice was tense, carrying the weight of recognition. "I remember the license plate. It's an ambush."

Nova's heart raced, and she drew in a deep breath, attempting to steady the nervous energy that flooded her. Anxiety surged as she mentally mapped out the potential outcomes. There was no avoiding it; they had to face this danger head-on.

In a swift, practiced motion, Nova slipped on a vest before emerging from the shelter of the SUV.

"US Marshals," she yelled with authority as she swung open the passenger-side door. "Get out of the truck with your hands up."

On the opposite side of the vehicle, River stood, gun drawn, moving cautiously toward the driver's side of the suspicious truck.

Nova repeated her command, scanning their surroundings, and that was when she noticed another truck strategically parked in front of the Lozano home, effectively blocking any chance of escape.

Pablo and Ramona Lozano were trapped.

The only thought on Nova's mind was finding a way to reach Arya's parents and get them to safety.

Just then, the passenger-side door of the vehicle that cut them off suddenly swung open, and a dark-skinned man with dreadlocks leaped out, brandishing a weapon aimed directly at her.

Instinct took over, and Nova fired off a shot with precision, hitting her target.

River swiftly closed the distance between them, pulling her to safety just as another assailant opened fire in her direction. He responded in kind, unleashing a round of gunfire.

The driver of the black truck, undeterred by the chaos, seized the opportunity to escape, accelerating around the other car with reckless speed.

Shots echoed through the air from the other vehicle before the driver shifted to Reverse and backed down the street.

River aimed and fired his weapon at the SUV.

Nova cautiously made her way to the bleeding man on the ground. She kicked his gun out of reach, then knelt to see if he was dead.

The Lozanos' SUV was bullet-ridden, its metallic frame

reflecting the faint glow of a single light bulb hanging from the ceiling. The passenger-side door hung open at an awkward angle, revealing torn upholstery and shattered glass.

Nova felt lightheaded. "Nooo!"

Ramona lay motionless on the cold concrete floor beside the vehicle, her chest rising and falling in shallow breaths. Pablo's lifeless body was sprawled out in front of the car, his limbs twisted at unnatural angles and blood staining the ground beneath him. The unmistakable scent of gunpowder lingered in the air, a grim reminder of the violence that had taken place.

She rushed toward them.

River ran behind her.

"Pablo Lozano is dead," he said, kneeling beside his body with his fingers over the pulse point.

Ignoring the tightening in her stomach, Nova checked on Ramona. "She's still alive." She pulled out her cell phone. "But she needs to get to a hospital." Nova called the shooting in and requested an ambulance.

Ramona opened her eyes. Her voice barely above a whisper, she said, "Please h-help…my d-dau…my daughter." She arched her back, winced and closed her eyes, probably trying to block out the pain.

"Mrs. Lozano, don't try to talk. The paramedics are on the way," Nova said "They should be here soon." She sent up a quick prayer, asking God to keep the woman alive. She didn't want Arya to lose both parents. One was devastating enough.

"Ava… Miami… GPS…"

"I'm going to do everything I can to help her."

"My h-husband…" Ramona murmured before losing consciousness.

Nova heard the wailing of a siren in the distance and released a short sigh of relief. She'd done what she could to help Ramona and now it was up to the medics.

While they waited for the EMTs, she peered inside the Lozanos' SUV.

Nova checked the GPS, took a photo of the address input for Miami. "So, you were planning to meet up with Arya," she whispered. "I knew you weren't telling me everything."

Police officers quickly arrived on the scene, followed by an ambulance.

River went over to talk to the police while she stayed with Ramona.

"She's been shot," Nova told the paramedic, ignoring the officers who were going over the details of what had happened with River. "One bullet grazed her arm and the other one…it's below her right breast. She's unconscious."

They placed the injured woman on a backboard and transported her to the ambulance.

"C'mon," Nova said. "We're going to Miami. That's where they were headed."

"You think Arya's there?"

She nodded. "Before she lost consciousness, Ramona asked me to help Arya and said the address was in the GPS."

Something flickered in River's eyes but disappeared as quickly as it had come, leaving Nova to wonder what he could be thinking.

"What is it?" she asked.

"I'm just wondering why she chose Miami."

"I don't know," Nova said. "But I'm calling the Marshals and having her mother placed under round-the-clock security."

River nodded, wrapping up with the police while Nova

called Cohen to update him. When she disconnected, she and River made their way back to their vehicle.

"Miami... I find it interesting that Arya would go there since there's tension between the Mancuso and Mali cartels in Miami," River said. "Johnny Boy's been trying to establish a firm presence down there."

She'd heard something about that. "The Mali cartel hijacked and burned more than a dozen stash houses belonging to the Mancuso cartel in Florida a year ago," Nova said. "The fighting between the two organizations was so bad that they had to impose a curfew in certain areas. There's definitely bad blood between those two."

"Maybe that's what Mateo had planned all along," River said. "If negotiating with Poppy and Johnny Boy didn't work, then it's possible he intended to sell information to the Mali cartel for protection."

"Only he didn't count on being murdered."

River nodded in agreement. "Exactly."

"He never learned his lesson," Nova said. "Let's hope Arya does."

Chapter Thirteen

Nova sent up a silent prayer for Ramona Lozano. She'd already called the Marshals office in Miami, giving them the address for Arya's known location and requesting round-the-clock protection. She and River would get there as soon as they could, and when they finally found her, Nova planned to be the one to convince her to come back into the program. One question lingered in her mind. "How did they find Arya's parents?"

"I don't know, but I'm glad we were there," River responded. "If we hadn't been, Arya's mother might be in the morgue with her husband."

"She's not out of the woods yet," Nova pointed out.

Her phone rang, and she answered quickly.

"The marshals are at the hospital," she announced after ending the call. "At least we know Ramona's safe. She's under twenty-four-hour security. As soon as she's stable enough, she'll be taken someplace safe to recuperate." Nova paused briefly, then said, "Looks like you've been right all along. The cartel must consider Arya a huge threat. There has to be a reason why. They must see her as more than a potential loose end."

River nodded. He made a call, then got off the phone, saying, "She's been assigned to a Victim Witness Coordinator. I'm expecting a callback from the federal prosecutor."

Nova couldn't help but express her disgust at such a heinous act. "Arya's going to be devastated over her father's death, but hopefully, the news about her mother will be a brighter note."

"My partner is going to meet us in Miami," River announced.

She grinned. "I'm surprised Kenny is still putting up with you."

River gave her a sidelong glance. "Did you really just say that?"

"The two of you fuss like an old married couple," Nova said. "Did y'all ever check into couples counseling like I suggested?"

He chuckled. "Whatever..."

IN THE DRIVER'S SEAT, Nova glanced over at River, who seemed deep in thought. She could tell from his body language that her nearness brought him discomfort. He always seemed to stand with his arms crossed as if to protect himself. Whenever River had his laptop out, he carried it close to his chest like a physical barrier. Even now, he sat with his back so straight that Nova couldn't imagine he was relaxed in that position. She tried a couple of times to strike up a conversation, but River gave her one-word responses.

They were both exhausted, so it didn't bother her that he wasn't being very talkative. However, Nova desperately wanted to bridge the gap that had formed between them. She was at a loss on how to do so. It was her fault that their relationship had crumbled, and she couldn't shake off the weight of guilt.

Despite everything, she knew that their priority right now was protecting the witness from the deadly drug cartel. If only they weren't in this dangerous situation, she could focus on repairing their broken bond.

As they crossed into Florida, Nova welcomed the short break. Her mind and body were drained from constantly being on high alert.

River offered to take over driving for the rest of the journey to Miami, and Nova didn't protest. Part of her wanted to stay awake and keep an eye on things, but exhaustion eventually caught up, and she drifted off for a quick nap.

Nova woke up to River softly humming a tune beside her. Blinking away the remnants of sleep, she looked out the window and saw they were parked in front of a small roadside café. The warm Florida sun was casting a golden glow over everything, lending an air of tranquility to the scene.

Stretching her limbs, Nova took a deep breath and turned to River. "How long have we been here?"

River glanced at her with a smile. "Just about half an hour. You seemed so peaceful—I didn't want to wake you."

Nova nodded gratefully, her heart swelling with affection for him. She realized that despite their strained relationship, there was still an unspoken connection between them.

"I feel refreshed. I can take over if you'd like to get some sleep." Nova glanced at the clock. "You haven't been to sleep since we left North Carolina."

"Let's grab something to eat, and I'll see how I feel after," he responded.

Stepping out of the car, Nova couldn't help but notice the way River's hand grazed against hers. It sent a thrilling rush through her body, but she pushed those feelings aside as they entered the café. She needed to focus on Arya and avoid getting lost in this unexpected attraction. The more time they spent together, the more Nova's resolve wavered, torn between duty and desire.

RIVER WAS DOING everything he could to maintain a professional distance around Nova. But after her statement, he realized it wouldn't be as easy as he'd imagined.

Memories of the last time they'd worked together came flooding back. River tried to force them back into the deep recesses of his mind. There wouldn't be a repeat of what had happened two years ago. River vowed he wouldn't succumb to the weakness he felt whenever Nova was in his presence. His self-control was much stronger now, built up by the heartbreak she'd inflicted upon him.

Nova wanted to move forward as if nothing had happened, but it wasn't that easy for River.

He glanced over at her. She was on the phone. She'd periodically checked in on Ramona Lozano to learn her prognosis. The last time she'd called the hospital, Ramona was in surgery.

"How is she?" he asked when she hung up.

"She's out of surgery and is expected to recover fully," Nova responded. "At least I'll be able to tell Arya that her mother will be okay despite her father's death."

River met her gaze. "I'm really sorry about your father."

"I miss him a great deal. My mom and I are also very close, but I am… I was a daddy's girl for sure. He was my hero."

"Is your mom still in Wisconsin?" River asked.

"Yeah," she answered, giving a slight nod. "She'll never leave Milwaukee. Since I left, she's visited me several times, but she loves her hometown. I tried to convince her to move to Charlotte." Nova turned in her seat. "I know you were very close to your grandmother."

"Adelaide was my heart." Memories of his time with her floated to the forefront of River's mind. "She didn't miss any of my games when I was growing up. She was the team mom… She hosted a lot of the meals…"

"She sounds wonderful," Nova said. "I didn't know my paternal grandparents—they disowned my dad for marrying a Black woman. But my mother's parents…Bessie and Isaiah Chapman… They gave me so much love that I don't feel I missed out on having the other set in my life."

"You can't miss what you never had," River responded. "That's what people say, but it's not true. I missed the love of a mother."

"I—"

He cut her off. "Let's change the subject." River hadn't meant to show more of his vulnerability, and he wouldn't open up to her about his relationship with his mother. They had crossed into a red zone. He had to get them back on course.

"Sure," Nova said.

River relaxed his body. They were once again in the safe zone, and he wouldn't stray from it again.

Chapter Fourteen

Nova moved her body into a more comfortable position. They were less than twenty minutes away from their destination. "Arya rented this place under her mother's name," she said, closing the laptop.

"I'm not so sure that was a smart move," River responded. "Since the cartel went after her parents."

"I emailed my supervisor about her mother. I'm hoping we can get Ramona into the program with Arya."

They took the exit SW 11th Lane, where the house was located.

River received a call from his partner.

"Kenny's already there," River announced when he ended the call. "Arya's in the house alone. She's expecting us.

"Nice location," River said as they passed through the small community of luxury homes.

Staring out the window, Nova said, "Mateo and Arya sure love the finer things in life. I thought she was going to faint when I took them to their house in Burlington. She kept saying it was much too small. They had a square-footage requirement of at least six thousand square feet."

"Okaay... What kinds of jobs did they have in the program?" River asked with a chuckle.

"She worked in a dental office," Nova said. "She was

the office manager. Her husband worked second shift at a medical-supply warehouse. Their incomes wouldn't have supported the type of housing they desired."

"We're here," River announced.

A pair of Arya's signature rosebushes led up to the porch.

Nova and River exited the vehicle and walked up the steps of the two-story house to the front door, which opened before they could knock.

Arya was standing in the doorway, immaculate from head to toe, but her eyes were lined with shadows, and she looked as though she hadn't slept in days. "Finally," she breathed as she guided them into the house. "I was beginning to worry you wouldn't find me." She led them into the living room.

"You didn't make it easy for me to find you," Nova began. "I found out from your mother."

"I thought my parents would be here by now. Do you know if they left already? They aren't answering their phones."

"Something's happened…" Nova began.

"What?" Her eyes grew large, and her voice trembled with fear.

"Arya, you might want to sit down."

But Arya refused, shaking her head frantically. "Nooo… Just tell me."

Nova took a deep breath and spoke the words that would shatter her world. "Someone from the cartel showed up at the house in Lake Glenville," she said gently. "Arya, they shot your parents."

She began crying.

"I'm so sorry. We couldn't save your father, but your mom is alive. Ramona's in a hospital under guard."

"It's all my fault," Arya sobbed. "I never should've involved them. Mateo told me to warn them and have them go to the vacation house and stay there until I was safe in Miami, and they could follow. But the day I left Burlington, I returned to the house because I'd forgotten something—I could see that someone had broken in, so I left."

"How did you end up at that abandoned house in Concord?"

She dropped down on the love seat. "Mateo found it. It's where I was supposed to stay until he returned." Nova and River sat across from her as she continued, "We were going to leave the country, but when I never heard back from him, I knew something must have gone wrong. I had a bad feeling... I knew he'd been killed. I didn't know what to do, so I called you. Then I was too scared to tell you where I was, so I left the phone behind." Arya shook her head. "I don't know how the cartel could track my parents down—they were careful in covering their tracks."

"They must have put some tracking software on the car or maybe they hacked your parents' phones," Nova suggested.

"If so, then it definitely won't be hard for them to find me, too," Arya said. "I spoke with my parents at least three or four times since leaving Burlington. It was because I didn't want them to worry." She chewed on her bottom lip. "Nova, I've really made a mess of things. Now my father is dead." She started crying again.

Nova leaned forward. "None of this is your fault."

Arya stood and paced across the hardwood floors. "Nova, I need to see my mother."

Nova shook her head. "I'm sorry, but it's unsafe for you to go there. The doctor will keep me updated on her progress."

"What if they try to kill her while she's at the hospital?"

"That won't happen."

"Why not?" Arya asked, knitting her trembling fingers together.

"Because they believe that she died along with your father," River interjected. "Your mother is being moved to a secure location under a temporary assumed name. US marshals are guarding her. Arya, she's safe."

Tears rolled down her cheeks. "I can't even bury my father."

"Your father will be cremated," Nova said. "Meanwhile, I'm working to get your mother into the program with you."

Arya appeared surprised. "You're not kicking me out?"

Shaking her head, Nova responded, "I'm giving you a second chance, but this time you will have to comply with the rules of WITSEC, and if you're holding on to evidence the DEA can use, you *must* turn in everything to Special Agent Randolph."

Arya averted her gaze. "I don't have anything. Mateo took it with him when he went to LA."

The hitch of her voice told Nova the woman was lying. Why?

"Arya, those are the terms," Nova stated. "It's not negotiable. We both know that Mateo was too smart to carry anything on him."

"I can't give you what I don't have. You can search my things for yourself." A lone tear ran down her cheek. "I wasn't involved in my husband's business. I just want a few minutes to myself to mourn the loss of my father. Can you give me that?"

Nova nodded. "Sure."

"I'll be in my bedroom."

"That went better than I thought it would," Nova said when she and River were alone in the living room. "She denies any prior knowledge of Mateo's business with the cartel."

"She knows more than she's telling us," River stated. "It's possible the information could also be somewhere in a bank, but I doubt it. Mateo didn't trust banks. He told the DEA how he'd hidden money in the walls of his office and the bottom of his freezer."

"Most likely, he was hiding that money from the cartel since he was stealing from them," Nova responded. "Didn't he turn over his computer to the DEA?"

"Yes," River responded with a nod. "Mateo was a smart man. I wouldn't be surprised if he had another computer hidden somewhere."

Kenny walked into the house after surveilling the perimeter of the property just as Nova said, "I'm going to check on Arya. I need to make sure she isn't trying to escape out the window."

"I don't think you have to worry about her," Kenny replied. "When I arrived, she appeared relieved. I believe she is grateful for the company and support during this situation."

"How is she?" River asked when Nova returned from checking on Arya. Kenny had picked up dinner for them from a popular chicken eatery.

"She says she's not hungry. Right now, she's still very emotional," she said. "Mateo and her father dead, her mother in the hospital, and the stress of being on the run. It's a lot to have to deal with. I was able to convince her to lie down and try to rest. She's worried that if the cartel was able to find her parents, they might be headed here."

"It's possible."

"I know," Nova responded.

"Does she have her cell phone?"

"Kenny took it from her," Nova said. "He turned it off."

"That's good to hear," River responded.

"He's camped outside her door right now," she stated. "I volunteered to take the next watch."

They found a movie to watch on television.

Nova stretched and tried to get comfortable. She snuggled up in one corner of the sofa.

When River glanced over at her, she was fast asleep. He'd known she wasn't going to last too much longer.

Smiling, he gave her a gentle nudge. "Why don't you go to one of the guest rooms? You're tired."

She sat up. "No, I'm good."

"No, you're not," River said. "Nova, you're exhausted."

She wiped her face with the backs of her hands. "I told Kenny that I'd keep watch so he could get some sleep."

"I can hold it down for now."

"Okay, but I just need a couple of hours," Nova stated.

Pointing toward the first-floor guest bedroom, River urged, "Go get in bed."

She refused. "No, I'll stay out here. Besides, I'm much too comfortable to move right now."

Grinning, he handed her a throw.

Nova smiled at him. "Thank you."

River settled back, keeping a watchful eye on their surroundings, as Nova drifted into a well-deserved rest on the sofa, the glow of the television casting a soft light on the room.

The night unfolded in a hushed ambience, punctuated by the occasional distant sounds of the city. He found a moment of respite, even amid uncertainty and danger.

NOVA WOKE UP with a start. She looked around, asking, "What time is it?"

"Almost two a.m.," River answered from across the room. He was in the dining area, working on his laptop.

"Oh, wow… I didn't mean to sleep so long."

"It's fine. You needed to get some rest, Nova. You're not a robot."

"Neither are you, River." Standing, Nova said, "I'll keep watch now. It's time for you to get some sleep."

He didn't argue. "I'm going to take a shower first. Wake me at six."

"Will do," she responded. "Where's Kenny?"

"He was in the kitchen a few minutes ago," River said. "He may be upstairs."

River opened the door to the first-floor bedroom and went inside, heading straight to the bathroom.

From where she sat, Nova could hear the steady downpour of water hammering the ceramic tiles inside the glass-enclosed shower.

She got up and navigated to the kitchen, needing something else to focus on than a wet, naked River Randolph. The hinges on the pantry door whined as she opened the door. She wasn't looking for anything specific but found cases of bottled water, various snacks, pasta and spaghetti sauce. In the refrigerator, Nova saw an assortment of cheeses, pepperoni, sausages and other meats.

Before she even turned around, Nova knew he was there. River was standing in the doorway, dressed in nothing but a pair of gray sweatpants. His look was so electrifying that it sent a tremor through her.

"Looking for a late-night snack?" he asked.

"Naw," Nova responded, averting her eyes. "I was just being nosy. What about you? I thought you were going to bed."

"I just came to get a bottle of water."

She retrieved one from the fridge and tossed it to him.

"Thanks," he said.

"Good night."

"What are you about to do?"

She swallowed tightly. "I'm going upstairs to check on Arya. I'll take the position outside her room."

He nodded. "I'm going outside to check the perimeter before I turn in."

Nova went upstairs and peeked in on Arya, who appeared to be sleeping soundly. Satisfied, she sat in the chair outside the room with her iPad. Might as well catch up on some reading, she decided.

She couldn't fully concentrate because of the handsome man in the room below. Seeing him in those gray sweatpants had struck a vibrant chord with her. She hadn't wanted to tear her attention from River but had forced herself to do so. Arya wasn't entirely out of danger yet.

Chapter Fifteen

"Where's our witness?" River asked the following day when he walked out of the bedroom. Although he hadn't slept eight hours, he felt completely rested in half the time.

"Probably still in bed," Nova responded as she removed four slices of bread from a toaster. "I haven't seen her at all this morning."

She walked the short distance to the fridge and retrieved the butter. "Kenny was down here a moment ago."

"You've got it smelling good in here."

She glanced over her shoulder at River. "You sound like you're surprised. I've been cooking since I was twelve. I'm a foodie, so I had to learn how to cook."

He held up his hands in mock surrender. "I didn't say a word…"

Nova went halfway up the stairs, then shouted, "Arya, if you intend to eat, you'd better come on down while everything is hot."

Arya entered the kitchen, saying, "I prefer to have breakfast in bed. I'm in mourning."

"I'll fix you a plate. You can take it upstairs if you want."

"I'm tired of tasteless food." She picked up a bagel. "I bought them like four days ago. Why can't we go to a real restaurant?" Arya whined.

"Because you're in hiding," Nova responded. "You're not out of danger yet."

"I'm so sick of this. This isn't how my life is supposed to go."

Nova shrugged. "Then you should've chosen a different one."

She glared at Nova. "Why did the feds take all our money? Why couldn't they leave us with at least a million?"

River could tell that Nova was struggling to keep her temper in check.

"It wasn't *your* money," River stated.

Arya rolled her eyes. "Mateo told me we would one day have our life back. He said we'd be rich again. That we could live anywhere in the world—it was our choice. We were going to buy a luxury yacht and live on it. Nobody would've been able to find us because we'd sail around the world... This just isn't fair."

"You should be grateful that you're still aboveground," Nova said. "Your life is in danger, Arya. We're not concerned with your social status. And while we're here, we're not your servants. We are here to keep you safe. Try to remember that."

Pouting, Arya rolled her eyes heavenward. She put a piece of toast on her plate, then stuck her fork into a sausage. "It would be nice to have an omelet now and then."

"Feel free to make one," Nova said with a grin to lighten the mood. "If you're cooking, I'll take one with spinach and tomatoes. Arya makes the best veggie omelets."

"I'm just saying... I feel like I'm owed something, Nova. I lost my husband because he went to the DEA for help, and now he's *dead*."

River opened his mouth to speak, but Nova touched his arm. When he met her gaze, she gave a shake of her head.

It was her telling him to take it easy on Arya.

After breakfast, they settled in the living room with Kenny posted at a window upstairs. Nova sat beside Arya on the leather couch while River sat in a chair across from them.

"I'm telling you that my husband wouldn't have given me any files or documents. Maybe he stored them in a safe somewhere, but only he would have the key."

They'd been trying to find out what the de Leons could be hiding but were getting nowhere. River decided to choose a different line of questioning. "I'm curious. What made you decide to come to Miami?"

Shrugging, Arya responded, "I don't know... I just thought I'd be safe here."

"In a city run by the Mali cartel?"

"Has nothing to do with me. I don't belong to any cartel."

She tried to keep her expression neutral, but River didn't miss the way she fidgeted on the couch.

"Your husband was a prominent figure in the Mancuso cartel. Was he going to switch sides?"

Arya shrugged once more. "I don't know."

River eyed her. "I decided to look into your mother's family, and one of your uncles was an attorney for the Mali family."

He heard Nova's soft gasp of surprise. He hadn't yet shared this piece of information with her. River had only found out that morning. He'd decided to look when he recalled that the owner of the property in North Carolina had a Florida mailing address.

"I don't know anything about that," Arya responded, her hands folded in her lap. "I mean, my uncle was a lawyer. He had his own law firm. No idea who his clients were."

"I have a feeling that Mateo knew all about him."

"My uncle died a long time ago." She met his gaze. "I

want to help you, but whatever my husband knew died with him, I'm afraid."

"Do you expect us to believe you had no help getting to Miami?" River demanded.

"I followed Mateo's instructions. That's all."

"Did you contact anyone outside of your parents?" River pressed.

Arya shook her head no. "Just the rental agency."

"Using your mother's identification," Nova said.

"It's all I had to work with. I don't have pay stubs or a job anymore. I needed a place to stay."

"Why don't we take a break?" Nova suggested.

River sighed, feeling frustrated with the lack of progress in his interrogation. He glanced at Nova, noting the sympathy in her eyes. She had always been compassionate and willing to give people the benefit of the doubt. But River knew better. He had seen firsthand the deceit and manipulation rampant in the criminal world.

Gesturing for Nova to follow him out of the room, he stepped into the foyer. Nova joined him, and they leaned against the wall, the air tense as their gazes locked in a silent conversation.

"We're not getting anywhere with her," River finally said with frustration. "She's hiding something. I can feel it."

"Agent Randolph thinks I'm lying," Arya said when Nova returned to the living room alone.

"Are you?" Nova inquired, fixing her with a penetrating gaze.

"No, I'm not," she retorted with a mixture of frustration and desperation.

"He's not the only one you have to convince," Nova stated, her tone indicating the gravity of the situation.

"What do you mean?" Arya's eyes widened with curiosity and a hint of fear.

"Johnny Boy. He knows your death was a lie… He's coming for you."

Arya's face lost color as she stammered, "Th-that's why I think it's time to leave Miami. Nova, just let me get a ticket to someplace far away. I'll disappear for good."

Nova shook her head, a heavy sense of responsibility settling on her shoulders. "He will hunt you down unless you help us put him in prison."

"Johnny Boy is unstoppable!" Arya exclaimed, her fear palpable. "Can't you see that?"

"We can't let fear dictate our choices. If you run, he wins. We need to stand up to him, expose the truth and make sure he pays for what he's done."

Arya looked torn, caught between the terror of facing Johnny Boy and the uncertainty of trusting Nova and the team to protect her. The gravity of their choices weighed heavily on them both, their fates entwined in this dangerous game that could only have one outcome—life or death.

Nova found River in the kitchen.

"How did it go?" he asked.

"She's scared."

"She doesn't trust that we can protect her," River stated. "We'll have to remind her that she and Mateo were safe until they left WITSEC. Johnny Boy knew exactly how to get Mateo to leave the program. Arya is not safe on her own."

"I agree." Nova sighed. "But how do we get her to trust us?"

SHORTLY AFTER MIDNIGHT, a vehicle parked across the street.

"There's a black SUV outside," Nova yelled from the home office. She watched with growing concern. "The doors are opening, and two guys just got out. River, they're *armed*."

"I'll get Arya," he said while taking the stairs two at a time.

Kenny went out the door leading to the back of the house. They were likely going to attack from both the back and front of the house.

Nova stood at the window, studying the men even as she slipped on a Kevlar vest. They didn't look familiar. The taller of the two was dressed in a black sweat suit, the expression on his face threatening. The other wore a black knit cap and leather jacket. He seemed intent on hiding his face.

River ran to the porch armed and ready while Nova went to the front window with her Glock pointed at the two men. River ordered them to halt.

Instead, the first assailant took aim.

The quiet street soon erupted in a deafening noise. Bright muzzle flashes and the sound of automatic gunfire filled the neighborhood, the bullets causing a couple of the windows to explode.

Nova ducked for cover, then fired at the would-be intruders, hitting the tall one. He collapsed on the sidewalk.

From the side of the house, Kenny took a shot at the other and wounded him in the arm. The man dropped his gun and stood with his good hand up in the air. Kenny approached to make an arrest.

Nova ushered Arya, who was in a Kevlar vest as well, downstairs and through the door leading to the garage. Her adrenaline was high, and she was ready to take on any threat.

She heard rather than saw the garage door going up.

Kenny gestured for them to leave. "Get out of here," he said. "I will take care of this." She slid into the vehicle beside Arya in the back seat while River got into the driver's seat.

"Arya, get down on the floor," Nova said.

The cartel gunman now lay on the ground with his hands stretched out. Kenny stood over him with his gun still in hand.

Arya was crying. She glanced over her shoulder and said, "How did they find me?"

"I wiped the address off the GPS in your parents' car, so I don't know, but I can promise you that they won't be able to find you again," Nova responded. "We're going off the grid."

River glanced into the rearview mirror at her as they drove away. "What do you have in mind?"

"I'm going to call Kaleb and Rylee. We could use their help."

"We need to change cars, too," he said.

She punched in a phone number.

They passed two police cars speeding toward the house.

"Kaleb, I need a favor," Nova said when he answered. "I need a safe place to take Arya de Leon. Someplace outside of Miami. She's been compromised." They could lie low and regroup using one of the houses that wasn't even on the Marshals' radar.

"Rylee's going to send Rolle to meet you in Jacksonville," he responded. "We'll let you know the address within the hour."

Nova looked over her shoulder at Arya. She sat in her seat, staring out the window blankly.

Maybe the poor woman is in shock.

"It's going to be a long night," River said.

"I'm glad we're all here to experience it still," she replied with a smile.

"I don't want to die," Arya said. Anguish colored the tone of her words.

"We're going to make sure that doesn't happen," River

stated. "We want you to live out the rest of your life without fear."

"I think I will always be afraid."

Nova was struck by how helpless Arya looked right now, and compassion washed over her.

She pulled a cap out of her backpack and held it out to Arya. "Put this on and keep your head low. I wouldn't put it past Poppy or Johnny Boy to have someone monitoring street cameras."

Arya twisted her long hair into a tight bun and secured it with a black scrunchie that was on her wrist. She put the cap on her head, then slipped on a pair of dark sunglasses.

Satisfied, Nova looked to the front.

"What about Kenny? He's going to meet up with us, right?"

River nodded. "I'll send him the location as soon as we get it."

THEY MADE IT safely to Jacksonville.

"We're supposed to meet Rolle at an IHOP off Stanton Road," Nova stated. She released a soft sigh of relief when they arrived. Rolle was there waiting for them as prearranged.

"Good to see y'all," he said when Nova got out of the SUV. "We're switching vehicles, so I'll take the keys to your SUV."

River handed them over. "Here you go. What are we driving?"

"This," Rolle responded while pointing to the car parked next to the SUV.

"Wow…nice…" River walked around the gray Mercedes G 550.

Rolle looked at Nova and asked, "You have the address for the safe house in Alabama?"

"Yeah," she responded.

"Then you're all set. Oh…" He pulled an envelope out of his pocket. "Kaleb sent this. He said that none of you should use credit cards. *Cash only.*"

Nova opened the envelope to reveal two thousand dollars in denominations of hundreds, fifties and twenties.

"Thanks for your help," River said.

"No problem. I was in Atlanta to visit my mom. Rylee called and I got on the first flight down here."

"Sorry for disrupting your vacation," Nova said.

"It's all good. I'm flying back home in a couple of hours. I had a day with my mom, so I'm good for another six months."

Nova glanced at River as they walked toward the car. "Why don't you get some rest and let me drive?"

He shook his head. "I'm good," he said before getting in and starting the car.

Nova sat down on the passenger side. "You just want to get behind the wheel of this Benz. I remember you telling me this was your dream car."

He chuckled. "I just thought you might want a break from driving."

"I'll take over in a couple of hours," she responded, settling into her seat and closing her eyes. "Wake me when you want me to take over."

"We're less than eight hours from Birmingham. I can make it."

"Good," Arya uttered. "I'm beginning to feel claustrophobic being in a car for so long."

Although Nova didn't voice it, Arya had more serious concerns than being cooped up in a car. The cartel had no intentions of giving up their search for her.

Chapter Sixteen

"Are you sure this is the right place?" River asked. He stared at the stunning brick home nestled in the prestigious Greystone neighborhood.

"This is the exact address that Kaleb gave me. 5430 Rosemont Circle in Birmingham."

"This house is gorgeous," Arya murmured. "*See*, this is the kind of place I should have in WITSEC."

"Not gonna happen," Nova responded with a chuckle. "The only way you get this type of house—you'll need a high salary to afford this lifestyle."

"Why couldn't I keep some of the money Mateo—"

Nova dismissed her words with a slight wave of her hand. "You already know the answer to that."

Arya sighed. "It isn't fair."

Kenny pulled up, parked and got out. River entered the house ahead of everyone and turned off the alarm. The main level featured a large gourmet kitchen with Corian countertops, a double oven, an eat-in area and a formal dining room. He navigated to the door leading to a screened-in porch with an open deck. The house was gated all around and separated from the other houses behind them by trees. He was pleased to see there were cameras and motion lights.

He joined Arya and Nova in the great room.

Nova pointed toward a hallway. "The master suite is over there," she told the men. "It has dual vanities, a jetted tub and a huge shower. Kaleb texted me some details on the way over."

"That's the room I want," Arya said.

River, Kenny and Nova all looked at her.

"No?"

"No," Nova stated. "Pick a room upstairs."

Listening to the interchange, River knew she was correct. Arya would be safer up there than on the main floor.

"This really sucks," Arya grumbled.

"I'll check out the second level," River said.

"I want to check out the grounds," Kenny stated.

River nodded and followed Nova and Arya upstairs, where they found four bedrooms, each with its own bathroom.

Arya chose the largest one, which came as no surprise.

"How long will we be here?" she asked.

"As long as necessary," Nova answered. "We're waiting on a new ID for you and a new location."

"And my mom will be able to come with me?" she asked.

"We're working out the details," Nova responded.

"Can't I go someplace exotic? I've had enough of small towns. I stand out like a sore thumb. I don't believe it's safe for me."

River returned downstairs and conducted a quick search of the kitchen to see if he had everything he needed in terms of cookware.

"What are you doing?" Nova asked when she strolled into the kitchen.

"I'm making dinner tonight," he announced. "Just checking to see if we have the cookware."

"Write down what you need and Kenny or I will pick it up," she offered.

River recalled the last time he'd made dinner for Nova. It was their last night together. He'd taken her to a restaurant owned by a friend of his. The restaurant was closed on Mondays, so they were the only people inside. She'd kept him company while he prepared their meals.

River forced his thoughts back to the present. This wasn't some romantic gesture on his part. He cleared his throat softly, then said, "Kaleb really came through with this house. It's a nice place."

She nodded. "He did. I already hate having to leave it."

He could feel her watching him as he typed up a shopping list for Kenny.

After a moment, she said, "I need to check in with my supervisor. Then I'm gonna check on Arya."

"I'll let you know when dinner is ready."

NOVA FOUND ARYA sitting on the edge of a king-size bed. Grief was etched all over her tear-streaked face.

"How are you holding up?" she asked.

The woman inhaled deeply. "I'm trying to put on a brave front, but I really miss my old life. I miss my father and Mateo… I'm scared all the time."

"We will do everything possible to make sure that you and your mother stay safe."

"Mateo told me he was going to fix everything so that the cartel would leave us alone."

"Did he tell you how he was going to accomplish this?" Nova inquired.

Arya hesitated, then said, "Agent Randolph was right. Mateo went to California to try and negotiate with the cartel. He said that if that didn't work, then he planned to give the Mali cartel information on the Mancuso operations in exchange for money and protection... I had a bad feeling about it, but Mateo... He just wouldn't listen to me."

"Why didn't you call me? I could've tried to talk some sense into Mateo."

"Because he made me promise not to say anything. He said we'd be gone before you realized it. Mateo said he had a plan." Arya started to cry again. "I—I t-told him not to trust those p-people. When he didn't respond to my texts or calls, I called my mother to tell her and Papi to go to the house on Lake Glenville. I thought they'd be safe there since no one knew about it."

"The cartel may have been listening to your mother's calls," Nova said.

Arya wiped her face before asking, "Can you call the hospital to check on my mother?"

"I can do that." Nova picked up her phone, connected with the nurse in charge of Ramona's care and spoke to her for a few minutes.

"Your mother is resting, and she's doing great," Nova said when she ended the call.

Arya released an audible sigh of relief. "Thank goodness." There was a brief pause before she spoke again. "Special Agent Randolph... He's very handsome, don't you think?"

"Let's focus on what's really important," Nova said. "Like telling him everything you know about the cartel."

RIVER HAD NOVA sample the chicken enchiladas after retrieving them from the oven.

"I'm impressed," she said. "Where did you learn to cook like this?"

"Trial and error," River responded. "Along with several cookbooks."

"Well, the enchiladas are delicious."

Nova helped him prepare the plates and carried them to the table.

After Kenny blessed the food, Arya sliced into her chicken enchilada and stuck a forkful in her mouth. "This is really good. Have you ever considered that maybe you're in the wrong line of work?"

"Cooking is a way to relieve stress. I'd never want to make it a career," River said. "I love my job with the DEA."

Wiping her mouth on a napkin, Arya said, "I was furious when Mateo told me he worked for the cartel. I always thought he should be working for some huge corporation. He was very intelligent. He could've worked anywhere he wanted."

"You really didn't know anything about Johnny Boy or Poppy Mancuso until you went into witness protection?" River asked.

Averting her gaze, Arya responded, "I didn't. Mateo didn't take me around his clients or business associates."

He glanced over at Nova, then turned to Arya again. "Your husband mentioned pulling all-nighters in his interview. You were never suspicious when he didn't come home? Most accounting jobs are Monday through Friday, and while some accountants work late, it's usually during tax season, and they aren't in the office all night long."

"Of course I was," Arya answered. "I thought he was having an affair. We fought about it all the time." She picked up her napkin and wiped her mouth again. "Can we change the subject, please? I don't want to talk about this anymore. Not right now."

River picked up his water glass and took a long sip. Arya's body language indicated that she wasn't being completely honest with him.

He was also finding it hard to keep his emotions at bay. It had been a long time since he'd been around Nova, and River wasn't prepared for how she made him feel.

Just being here in this room with her sent a course of electricity within him. River tried to shake off this feeling of being so alive, but he failed miserably. The part he thought had died rose in him suddenly and refused to be ignored.

After they finished their meal, Kenny volunteered to clean the kitchen and, surprisingly, Arya offered to help him.

When they were done and had gone upstairs, River and Nova settled in the loft.

"Kenny's going to come up and relieve you at midnight," River announced. "I'm probably going to crash. I'm tired."

"You should," she responded with a smile. "Thank you again for such a delicious dinner. It was a lot better than the pizza I thought we'd be eating tonight."

River met her gaze and couldn't look away, feeling that there was a deeper significance to the visual interchange. He pulled Nova toward him and kissed her, surprising them both. Heat sparked in the pit of his stomach and ignited into an overwhelming desire.

He kissed her a second time; his tongue traced the soft fullness of Nova's lips. His mouth covered hers hungrily until he released her, saying, "I'm sorry. I never should've done that. I have no idea what came over me."

Nova chuckled. "If we'd had wine, we could blame it on that."

"I suppose we could pretend that the kiss never happened," River suggested.

She gave a stiff nod. "Yeah, we could do that."

His senses reeled as if short-circuited, but he tried to

display an outward calm despite the physical reactions to his desire for Nova. "Maybe we should get back to the reason why we're here."

She agreed.

"I really didn't mean to ravish you like that."

Nova placed two fingers to his mouth and said, "We're fine, River. I have no illusions that the kisses meant anything to you."

"That's not…"

"Good night, River. I'll see you in the morning."

Instead of going to bed like he'd planned, River went down to the office.

He checked the security camera footage displayed on the monitor. He was sure they were safe and hadn't been found, but he intended to stay cautious.

He checked every area more than once.

After conducting a walk-through to make sure the windows and exterior doors were securely locked, River turned on the alarm system before going to the great room. He sank down on the sofa to watch television. He kept the TV volume low.

River felt himself drift off and forced his eyes open. He got up, went to the office, then checked the security cameras once more before navigating to the bedroom to shower.

Afterward, he considered going upstairs to check on the women but pushed the thought away. He didn't want to face Nova just yet. River had given in to his emotions earlier, but it couldn't happen again. He didn't want a repeat of the last time they were together.

Chapter Seventeen

Positioned in the loft across from where Arya lay sleeping, Nova remembered the kisses she'd shared with River over and over in her mind for most of her watch.

She squirmed uncomfortably in the chair she was sitting in. Her back was starting to ache, and every now and then there was numbness in her legs.

Nova stood up and stretched.

She thought she heard movement below and crept over to the railing, looking down. She watched as River strode to the narrow window beside the door and peered outside. He'd changed into a pair of light gray sweats. The socks on his feet cushioned the sound as he walked across the marble floor.

She descended the stairs, whispering loudly, "Is everything okay?"

River turned to face her and said, "I thought I saw lights through the trees. It looked like the vehicle was coming here, but then it turned around. Nobody's out there."

Alarmed, Nova walked over to a window and glanced out. "Are you sure?" Kaleb's brother, Nate, owned the safe house and the adjacent properties on both sides. She was confident that the cartel couldn't have discovered their location.

River nodded. "I am."

She relaxed. "That's good to hear."

"Why don't you go back up there and get some sleep?"

"I'm good," she said while trying to stifle another bout of yawns. "You were supposed to be resting."

"I wasn't as sleepy as I thought," River said. "If you want, you can take the master suite down here and I'll keep watch."

"Kenny should be up taking over shortly."

Nova was touched by his concern but didn't allow herself to think it could be something more. What they'd shared two years ago had been nice. She cherished the memories of their time together, but the reality was that they would both do their jobs, and when Arya and her mother were safe, she and River would say their farewells and that would be the end of it.

"You really need to get some rest," Nova said.

"I will at some point." He smiled, and she couldn't deny the sudden warmth she felt being on the receiving end of that smile. "Good night, Nova."

"Good night."

"I HAVE SOMETHING to tell you both," Arya announced when she came downstairs the next morning.

"What is it?" Nova asked as she poured herself a cup of herbal tea.

"I think it's time I told you the truth," she said, settling across from Nova at the breakfast table. "It's true. Mateo had enough stuff on the cartel to cause some serious damage."

Nova nodded. "What made you change your mind?"

"It finally sunk in that Johnny Boy isn't going to stop until he finds me."

Nova rested her hands on the table. "I'm not going to let that happen, Arya."

River and Kenny joined them a few minutes later.

"Arya wants to talk to you both," Nova stated.

She nodded. "I know all of you will do what you can to keep me safe, but Johnny Boy means to kill me. At least you'll know everything if that happens."

"I meant what I said," Nova told her. "We are going to protect you with everything we have."

Despite the danger seemingly all around them, this was the very thing that Nova had trained for—she was willing to risk her life to save Arya. She'd followed her father's path to become a marshal because it was admirable work. Nova also thought it took courage to enter the witness protection program—having to be separated from loved ones, often living in strange cities, then having to lie to everyone and look over a shoulder for the rest of the individual's life. Arya was doing the right thing.

Nova took a sip of her tea. "The best chance for being safe is following my instructions, Arya. And by telling River everything you know."

Arya carefully opened the silver locket hanging from her neck and extracted a small, black micro SD card. She held it out to River with a determined look in her eyes.

Nova couldn't believe it—all the evidence to bring down the cartel was in his hands.

"It's all there. Some of the information you already have, but there was a whole lot more that my husband didn't give the DEA all those times he met with them."

"I knew it," River exclaimed.

Nova left Arya alone in the room with River and Kenny. She went to the office and eyed the quad split screen, checking the multiple security cameras on the property. Although she was confident that they wouldn't have any unwanted visitors, Nova wanted to be prepared if there were any signs of suspicious activity on the property. Her Glock was loaded and ready.

She made another call to the hospital requesting an update on Ramona Lozano.

"Mrs. Lozano's wounds are healing nicely," Nova was told.

Arya's mother had been moved to another location, which would be safer for her. "Have there been any calls asking about her?"

"No, ma'am."

"That's good to hear."

Nova found a couple of articles online about the deaths of Pablo and Ramona Lozano. She printed them. She wanted to prepare Arya before she found them herself.

RIVER SLIPPED THE SD card into his laptop while Arya picked up an apple and took a bite out of it. He'd spent the past hour being filled in on what Arya knew and now he wanted to dive into the evidence. His eyes widened as he realized that all the evidence they needed against the powerful cartel was contained on that small card.

As he scrolled through the files, Arya said, "You now have everything, Special Agent Randolph. More financial records, lists of properties owned by the cartel—even drug shipments."

"Mateo kept meticulous records," he said. River was relieved to have this information and someone else who could testify.

"So, what do you think?" Nova asked when River entered the office an hour later. "Can you use any of what she gave you?"

"We have some solid and damaging evidence," he answered. "I can see why Mateo tried to blackmail Poppy.

This information could potentially topple a huge part of her dynasty. However, it's going to be a challenge getting to her since she's hiding on a private island near Ecuador and there is no extradition to the United States."

"I believed Arya when she told me that Mateo kept her out of the loop. She lied to me."

"She was protecting her husband."

"I'm beginning to think she knew all along that Mateo worked for the Mancuso cartel."

"I've always believed that," River said.

"Where is she?" Nova asked.

"She's still in the dining room with Kenny."

"I checked in with the hospital. Her mother's doing well."

"You should tell her," River said. "I need to make some phone calls. Mind if I sit in here?"

Nova pushed away from the desk. "It's all yours. By the way, I checked the security cameras—nothing unusual." She placed a hand on her weapon.

"Keep an eye on Arya," River said. "I'll be out shortly."

Nova left the office.

He called his supervisor first, then the federal prosecutor to update. "I have great news. I have the rest of the information DeSoto didn't turn over to us earlier. I'll email everything over to you in a few minutes."

River was grateful to Nova. He knew that she was part of the reason Arya had agreed to come forward.

Chapter Eighteen

After Arya went to bed, Nova and River sat down on the stairs.

She'd been wanting to have another conversation with him, but thought it best to wait for an opening. He gave her that when he said, "I keep thinking about the night you came to my hotel room. You could've talked to me about your feelings, Nova. You didn't have to run away. Your silence and absence spoke volumes."

"I realize that I handled things wrong," she responded. She wanted to be completely honest with River. "When we first got together, I didn't think either of us was looking for anything serious."

"So, you were just in it to have a good time—nothing more?"

She looked over at him. "I'm not saying that at all, River."

"Then exactly what are you saying?"

"We lived over three thousand miles apart. I really didn't have any preconceived notions about what was going on between us. I knew that neither one of us wanted a relationship that might interfere with our jobs—remember we talked about that? It's probably why I honestly never expected you to make any type of declaration. Especially so soon."

"To be honest, I surprised myself when I said it," River

confessed. "I have to admit that I never expected things between us to become so passionate. It scared me, too, but I was willing to take a chance with you. I thought you felt the same way."

"That's why I regret leaving. I wish more than anything that I'd just talked to you that night."

"I wish you had," he responded. "I've had to deal with rejection all of my life and it's not been easy for me to trust someone with my heart." River wished he could rescind the words that had just come out of his mouth. He hadn't meant to share his personal pain with her. Not like this. He didn't want her pity.

She reached over and took his hand in her own. "I'm really sorry."

River gave a slight shrug. "You don't have to apologize."

"Yes, I do," Nova insisted. "You deserved better than what I gave you."

"I appreciate that you didn't lie about your feelings."

"You must know that I cared deeply for you, River. And since we're being honest… I didn't realize just how much until after I left."

He gave a wry smile. "It's all in the past now."

Nova swallowed hard, then said, "I've really missed talking to you."

River eyed her. "Same here."

"Do you think we can try being friends?" she asked.

"Sure. If that's what you want."

She nodded. "I'd really like that."

His cell phone rang. "I need to take this call." River stood up and walked down the stairs.

NOVA SAT THERE wondering if he was going to come back upstairs. When ten minutes passed, she got up and moved to the loft.

At some point, she must have fallen asleep, because when Nova woke up, it was around 2:00 a.m. Kenny was seated in a chair across from her. He was watching something on his phone.

He glanced over at her and smiled.

Nova got up and checked on Arya, then crept down the staircase. She was hungry.

She was surprised to find that River was still up.

"When I finally got off the call, you were asleep," he said.

"I'm really glad we had a conversation," Nova responded while looking for something to snack on. "I know it doesn't change anything."

"It doesn't change things, but we don't have all that tension between us any longer." He opened the refrigerator. "There's some fruit, cheese and crackers."

"You must be snacky, too."

"I had an apple. I finished it just before you came down."

Leaning against the counter, Nova asked, "River, what did you mean when you said you've been dealing with rejection all your life?"

His expression became unreadable. "It's nothing."

"Please don't do that. *Talk to me.*"

"My mother never wanted me," he announced. "After I was born, she left me with her mother. She was only sixteen at the time, so my grandmother raised me. She got married when she was twenty, but even before that…I don't remember having a real relationship with Mary—that was her name. I think back then she was like a sister to me."

Nova's heart broke at the thought of River having to grow up feeling rejected by his mother. She couldn't imagine what that was like. "And you two were in the same house?"

River nodded. "There were a few times when she'd help me with my schoolwork… She'd buy me a toy every now and then, but that was it. After she got married, Mary and her husband had a baby girl. They loved Bonnie dearly. I think Mary always wanted a girl."

"She never came back for you?" Nova asked.

"No. I was never in Mary's heart. I was only an inconvenience to her."

"Did her husband know that she was your mother?"

"My grandmother told him. He welcomed me, but Mary told him that her mother refused to part with me."

Nova hurt for River. "I'm so sorry."

His gaze downcast, he shrugged in nonchalance. "It's fine. I had a wonderful grandmother and she loved me until the day she died."

Nova reached for his hand, which had settled near hers, then thought better of making contact. They were still in a fragile state. "But I'm sure it hurts that your mother rejected you. Is she still alive?"

"Mary died about six months ago."

"Did you attend her funeral?"

"I did, but only because Bonnie said she needed me to be there with her," River responded.

"You and your sister have a good relationship, then?" Nova inquired.

"Yes, we do. I'm thankful that Mary didn't try to discourage my getting to know Bonnie. I love my sister."

They walked across the hall to check the security cameras.

"So far, so good," she murmured. "I spoke with Sabra earlier, and from what she's gathered from cartel conversations, Johnny Boy is furious with his men for losing the package." Sabra was a tech on the task force Rylee had put together, and her intel had been helpful.

"That's pretty much what I expected," he responded. "That SD card Arya handed over is a definite threat to his organization. I feel good knowing that he's most likely losing sleep over this."

"I'm with you there," Nova said. "Every time I think of Calderon in prison for the rest of his life plus one hundred and thirty-five years…it makes me really happy. Although he didn't actually shoot my father, he is still responsible. I wonder how he feels about being so easily replaced by Johnny Boy as Poppy's right hand."

"You have a right to your feelings, Nova." River paused a moment, then asked, "Are you wanting to leave the Marshals because of your father?"

"That's a part of it."

River wrapped his arms around her, drawing her closer in his embrace. With her body pressed to his like this, he felt blood coursing through his veins like an awakened river.

Their eyes locked as their breathing came in unison.

Nova tried to ignore the aching in her limbs and the pulsing knot that had formed in her stomach.

Without a word, River swept her up, weightless, into his arms.

He carried her to the first-floor bedroom, where he eased her down onto the bed.

He unbuttoned her blouse, but before River could go any further, he abruptly pulled away, saying, "I'm sorry. I can't do this to myself a second time."

His rejection was like a bucket of cold water, washing over Nova and cooling her ardor.

"It's okay," she said while buttoning up her top. "I understand."

But the truth was that she didn't understand at all.

Nova looked up at him, noting his pain-filled gaze. "You're just not ready."

"You are such a beautiful woman. I…"

"It's okay." She shrugged. "Why don't we just keep this at friendship?"

He nodded. "I'm sorry."

"Stop apologizing, River. It's not necessary." Nova wanted him to know that he didn't need to protect himself from her. Not this time. "I've always cared about you."

"Let's not do this…"

"We're supposed to be having an honest conversation." She really wanted him to hear her heart through her words.

"And I'm speaking in truth."

"So am I," Nova said. "I just need you to listen and hear me."

"I can't do this right now," he responded. "I'm sorry."

He walked out of the bedroom.

"No," she whispered, "I'm sorry."

RIVER WOKE UP from a dream about Nova that had quickly become erotic. He turned from one side to the other, trying to escape thoughts of her, but it wasn't meant to be. She was still heavy on his mind.

He had thoroughly enjoyed spending time with her in the early morning hours. For a moment, River had been able to forget that so much time had passed between them. It felt like old times.

Nova never did anything to try to impress him—she was comfortable in her own skin, which was a quality he greatly admired.

When River thought of how he'd reacted last night, he felt like a heel for running out on her. He should have just explained that he felt it was best to have a platonic relationship. He never should have gotten involved with her on a personal level. From the moment River saw her that first time, he'd known that his life would never be the same.

"I should have kept it business between us," he whispered. "From the very beginning."

It was too late then and it was too late now.

River was still in love with her.

Chapter Nineteen

Nova hoped to avoid River, but he opened the door to the room he'd slept in just as she walked by.

"Good morning," she said, not looking at him. "I'm glad you finally got some sleep."

"I'm sorry about last night."

She shrugged in nonchalance. "Forget about it. I have." Nova wasn't about to let him know how much his rejection hurt.

His eyebrows arched a fraction at her words. The air suddenly felt thick with tension between them as they went downstairs.

River followed her into the kitchen and tried to make small talk, but Nova didn't have much to say.

"Nova…"

"I mean it," she interjected. "Let's just forget about it."

"It's not that easy for me," he responded.

"That sounds like a *you* problem," she said, walking over to the refrigerator and retrieving the carton of eggs. She was embarrassed and just needed some distance.

River left the kitchen without another word.

Nova was relieved because she needed some time alone to process her feelings. She could no longer deny that she was falling in love with him.

She cooked several slices of bacon, scrambled six eggs and made four slices of toast. When everything was ready, she went upstairs.

Nova ran into Arya coming out of her bedroom. "I was just coming to tell you that breakfast is ready."

She stopped by the office. "Breakfast is ready," she told River and Kenny.

Ten minutes later, they all sat at the table, eating in silence.

River was the first to finish his food.

Pushing away from the table, he said, "I'll be in the office if you need me."

She nodded, then reached for her glass of orange juice and took a sip. Kenny left a moment later.

"Nova, I'm sorry for lying to you after everything you've done to keep me safe," Arya said when they were alone. "Mateo really thought he could get the cartel to back off. He went to Los Angeles to meet with Poppy. He figured she'd do anything to get that information back."

Wiping her mouth, Nova said, "Like I told you before, you should've come to me. If you had, I would've done everything I could to keep him safe, even if it meant holding him in custody."

Arya leaned back in her seat. "I have to live with the choices I've made for the rest of my life. I've lost two important men in my life. I pray I don't lose my mother. I don't think I could bear it."

"If there's anything else that you know about the cartel, you should tell River and Kenny."

"I will," she responded. "Because there is more."

Stunned, Nova met her gaze. "Are you telling me that you're still withholding evidence?"

"I've given him all the files. I just didn't tell him everything that I know yesterday."

"This isn't a game, Arya."

"I know that."

Nova called out for River and Kenny to join them.

"What's going on?" they asked in unison.

Arya appeared slightly embarrassed before admitting, "I need to tell you—"

"If you're going to confess that you knew he was working for the cartel, I figured as much," River interjected.

Kenny put his phone on the table. He was recording the conversation.

"I've always known about my husband's relationship with members of the cartel…" She glanced over at Nova before adding, "That's because I urged him to work for them."

Nova's mouth dropped open. She hadn't expected to hear anything close to this.

"You have to understand…" Arya continued. "My parents weren't supportive when my husband and I married. They didn't think he was good enough for me and refused to give us any financial support. We were so poor at the time, and I didn't want to live that way. I knew my uncle worked for the Mali cartel and I wanted what my cousin had… Glitz and glamour…fancy parties and private jets. I wanted it all."

Arya clasped her hands together and hid them in the folds of her ruffled maxi skirt. "My husband was a small-time drug dealer when we met in college. My friend connected him with her boyfriend and soon he was working for the Mancuso cartel. After he graduated, he moved up the ranks and started handling the money." She paused a moment, then said, "My background is also in accounting, although I also had a real estate license. On occasion,

I'd help him reconcile the books, usually around the end of the year. I'd also help him find opportunities to launder the money."

Floored, Nova glanced over at River, who said, "What you're telling me is that you also worked for the cartel."

"Yes," she responded. "I found property for them. The cartel owns a building on Front Street in Los Angeles. It used to be a clothing store. There's nothing there now, but according to the paperwork filed at the end of the fiscal year, it's bringing in over a hundred thousand in sales each month."

"Are you telling us that they're laundering money through a store that's closed?" River asked.

Arya nodded, then said, "That's not the only one. They have several businesses like that—empty storefronts that show a profit on the books. They buy lots of commercial properties. Houses, too. They also have several legitimate businesses. A nightclub on Sunset Boulevard, a couple of hair salons and beauty-supply stores. They own several shell corporations, but the largest is Grupo Worldwide Holdings Inc."

Nova sat there listening to the woman she'd believed to be an innocent victim in all this.

"Have you ever been around Johnny Boy?" River inquired.

"Once," she responded. "And I'm sure it was really him. Not one of the fake Johnnys."

"Why do you say that?" he asked.

"Because he had a tattoo of his father on his chest with the initials *CR* below it. Six months before they discovered we were stealing from them, we were invited to a pool party at one of his houses. The host was supposed to be Johnny Boy. Only he wasn't the host. He was just another guest.

At least, he pretended to be one. I'd drunk a lot and had to go to the bathroom, and when I came out, I glimpsed this guy in one of the bedrooms with some girl. He didn't have on a shirt. That's when I saw the tattoo. It's pretty large."

"Did he see you?" Nova asked.

"I don't think so. I got out of there as quickly as I could, because if he had, I'd probably be dead already."

"Why didn't you tell us any of this before?" River asked.

"Because Mateo was trying to keep me safe," she responded. "I hope you get Johnny Boy. *I hope he dies.*"

"Is there anything else you can tell us?" Nova inquired.

"I've told you everything. The rest is on that SD card." Arya paused a moment, then said, "I never even told Mateo about seeing that tattoo. I couldn't risk anyone finding out that I could identify Johnny Boy. I want to stay far away from these people—they've destroyed my life." She looked at River. "I don't want to have to testify."

"We can request anonymity," he responded. "If granted, none of the defendants will know who you are."

"If you can really do that, then I will testify to what I know," Arya said, "but I'm hoping that with the information and evidence you have in hand, you won't need me at all."

"I can't make any promises. I will need to speak with the federal prosecutor about all this."

"I understand."

"Arya, we will do everything we can to ensure you're safe," River said.

Arya glanced at Nova. "I hope you'll be able to get my mom into the program with me. If she's with me…we can completely disappear together." Arya stretched, asking to retreat to her bedroom for some rest. River nodded.

After she left, Nova said, "If Arya never told Mateo

about the tattoo, then Johnny Boy may have no idea that anyone outside of his small circle knows about it."

"I'm glad she finally decided to come clean." River shook his head. "I had no idea just how involved she was. She worked for the cartel."

"Makes sense to me why they're after her," Kenny said.

Kaleb called Nova later that afternoon. "We've heard some chatter. Johnny Boy isn't a happy man these days. He wants his lost package found. He's now offering bonuses to the person who finds it."

"Arya knows too much. She can also identify Johnny Boy. She's going to need round-the-clock security until his arrest."

Kaleb agreed.

The next few days went much the same. Cohen gave his approval to keep Arya in Birmingham for now. After breakfast, Arya rehearsed her new backstory in the WITSEC program; they took an hour and a half for lunch, then more practice to perfect her new identity. After dinner, Arya spent an hour or so with River and Kenny, discussing her time in the cartel.

Nova thought about how much she would miss working with the Marshals Service, but she was super excited about the next chapter in her career. Her eyes strayed to River.

If only she had someone to share it with.

River went outside after Arya went upstairs to her room after dinner one night.

Nova found him sitting on the patio half an hour later. They hadn't talked about what had almost happened a few nights ago or how it made her feel.

"I realized something from the other night," she said. "I fully understand how you must have felt when I left without saying anything to you. I want to apologize for that, River."

He met her gaze. "Apology accepted."

He was still peering at her intently. Nova saw the heart-rending tenderness of his gaze. She secretly hoped that River would ask her to stay outside a while longer, but he didn't, much to her disappointment.

"I'll see you tomorrow morning," she said.

"G'night."

Nova tried to swallow the lump lingering in her throat.

She was falling in love with a man who would never be able to return that love. The thought shattered her heart into a million little pieces.

RIVER STOOD OUTSIDE the room Nova was in. He'd been there for almost ten minutes before finally deciding to knock.

She opened the door, then stepped aside to let him enter.

"Tomorrow, Arya and I will travel to meet with the marshals transporting her mother," Nova announced. "Her documents will arrive in the morning. I don't want to prolong this any longer."

River nodded in understanding. "She won't be in your custody after that."

"I know. I might even miss her."

They stood staring at one another with longing. There was no denying that they shared an intense physical awareness of each other.

Without warning, River pulled Nova into his arms, kissing her. He held her snugly.

"I'm so glad you're here."

He gazed down at her with tenderness. "I will be here for as long as you need me."

Parting her lips, Nova raised herself to meet his kiss.

His lips pressed against hers, then gently covered her mouth. River showered her with kisses around her lips and along her jaw. As he roused her passion, his own grew stronger.

This time, it was Nova who slowly pulled away. She took him by the hand and led him over to the edge of the bed.

They sat down.

"Being around Kaleb and Rylee reminds me of how much I'm lacking when it comes to love," Nova said. "I've never admitted this to anyone, but I get lonely sometimes."

"So do I," River confessed. "Growing up, I used sports to take my mind off how lonely I felt. Now I use work."

His closeness was so male, so bracing.

River stroked her cheek. "What are you thinking about?"

"You want the truth?" she asked.

He nodded.

"I was thinking about how long it's been since I've been this close to a man. How long it's been since I've kissed a man or made love." She raised her eyes to meet his. "It's been a while."

"Same here," River murmured.

"I'm not trying to seduce you," she said quickly. "I meant what I said about us being friends."

"I was thinking about hanging around in Charlotte for a few more days when we get there. I can change my plane ticket. That is if you don't mind showing a friend around the city."

She broke into a grin. "I don't mind at all."

He reluctantly and quietly made his way to the door and eased it open. "Good night."

It was getting harder and harder to walk away from Nova.

Chapter Twenty

Nova's mission was a simple, protective security detail: take Arya to the checkpoint, hand her off to the next set of marshals who would settle her in her new location, and head back to Charlotte.

They were nearly in Tennessee—Nova had accompanied another marshal in moving Arya securely to the handover point. "How is everything going?" River asked when she called to check in while at a gas station.

"It's going. I've considered taping Arya's mouth up a few times," she admitted. "We're about thirty minutes away from the destination."

He chuckled. "Exercise patience, beautiful."

"I'm trying," Nova said. "After the handoff, I'm heading straight to the airport. I'll get home close to six."

"I'll see you then."

His words brought a smile to her lips. "Same here."

When she hung up, Arya said, "I knew something was going on between you and Special Agent Randolph."

Nova didn't respond. She slid back into the passenger seat, next to the marshal who was transporting them.

When they passed the sign welcoming them to White Water, Tennessee, Arya said, "I don't think anybody will ever think to look for me here. I've never even heard of this place. It looks kinda depressing."

"That's the idea," she responded. "We don't want anyone to find you."

"What is there to do in White Water? And where is there to shop to find *real* clothes? I'm not a Target kind of girl."

"The town is close to Memphis," Nova responded. "It's a thirty-minute drive. But, Arya, you really must be careful. You can't forget for one minute that Johnny Boy wants to silence you permanently."

"That's good to know about Memphis." Arya looked out of the passenger window. "As for that murderous Johnny Boy…I hope somebody kills him."

"Thanks to you, we now have a good shot at finding the man."

"I wish I didn't have to have another handler."

Nova hated having to turn her charge over to someone else, but it was for the best. "You'll be fine, and I think you'll really like him," Nova reassured her. "Just follow the rules… You and your mom will be safe."

Arya nodded. "It's been a painful lesson to learn."

Nova glanced over at the marshal who was driving them, and smiled. She truly hoped Arya was serious.

"I appreciate you letting me pick out my new name. I've always loved the name Ariel. *Ariel Ramos.* I love it."

"Glad to hear it," she replied with a smile.

"Will my mother be there when we arrive? Sorry…I mean my aunt Rosa."

Nova looked out the front passenger window. She'd been checking periodically to make sure they hadn't picked up a tail. "If not, she should be arriving shortly."

"I can't wait to see her."

Nova released the breath she was holding when they arrived at the designated meeting location. She opened the door. "Stay inside," she told Arya. Hand on her duty weapon, she walked around to check the perimeter.

Deputy Marshal Hightower, who'd driven them, remained near the vehicle.

They were the first to arrive.

Nova walked back to the SUV and got back inside. "They should be arriving soon."

"You don't think anything happened to them?" Arya asked.

"Nothing outside of traffic, maybe."

An SUV like the one they were in pulled up a few minutes later.

Arya reached for the door handle. "Why aren't we getting out?"

"Just wait," Nova uttered.

Hightower got out of the vehicle first and walked over to talk to the driver of the other SUV.

"You can get out now," she confirmed.

Nova escorted Arya over to the waiting vehicle, which held Ramona. Nova's eyes watered at the emotional reunion between mother and daughter, who would now live as aunt and niece.

When they were back in the SUV, she said, "Drop me off at the airport in Memphis, please."

Nova eagerly anticipated going back home and reuniting with River. She was thankful for the opportunity to mend their friendship, but she wasn't expecting too much. After all, she was the one who had left. But she'd apologized for the past. Now it was up to River to take the next step.

DESPITE HER RESERVE, Nova threw herself into River's arms the moment he arrived at her house. "I'm so happy to see you."

She'd called him as soon as her plane landed, then rushed home to shower before his arrival.

"Same here," he responded, sweeping her into his arms. His mouth covered hers hungrily.

Nova gave herself freely to the passion of his kiss before stepping out of his embrace to say, "Let's get business out of the way first. Your witness and her mother are safe and secure in their new location." She handed him a business card from her pocket. "Here is the contact of her new case agent. For the next two weeks, they'll have twenty-four-hour security and stay in a safe house before moving to their new home."

"Thank you," he said.

"Where's Kenny?" she asked.

"Hanging out with some of the local DEA agents. He wanted to enjoy himself before his flight back to LA."

Nova chuckled. "I'm sure. It feels good to breathe finally," she said. "I like Arya, but I'm thrilled that someone else is responsible for her. She's more cunning than I ever thought."

"I agree."

"And right now, she's the only person who can potentially identify Johnny Boy."

Nova poured two glasses of red wine, then handed one to River.

After preparing plates laden with cheese, crackers, pepperoni and hot-and-spicy chorizo, they sat down on the sofa.

"I don't feel like I can fully relax until Johnny Boy's off the streets," Nova said. "Poppy will still be out there somewhere, though. Once I close out this WITSEC case, I'm turning in my resignation and going after them both."

River took a sip of wine, then bit into a cracker covered with cheese and pepperoni. "You'll be a great asset to Rylee's team."

"I think so," Nova responded.

River's phone rang.

"You've got to be kidding me…" she muttered, sitting up. "Tell Kenny he has terrible timing."

"It's not him," he responded.

Nova nodded and gave him some privacy. She went to her office and quickly checked her email.

River appeared in the doorway moments later. "Johnny Boy's been located. Kenny and I have to catch an early flight to Arizona in the morning."

She couldn't contain her excitement. "Where is he?"

"He's hidden in some remote hideaway between Arizona and the Mexican border," River stated. "Kenny and I will participate in his capture as part of the Native American Targeted Investigation of Violent Enterprises Task Force. They're called NATIVE for short."

Nova knew of the group. Her father had first told her of the elite group of Native American trackers working within US Immigration and Customs Enforcement. The team patrolled their portion of the border between Arizona and Mexico in the fight against drug and human trafficking. "You'll be working with the Shadow Wolves, then," Nova said.

"You know about them?"

"My dad told me about them. Have you worked with them before?"

"I have," River said. "One of their team members, Ray Redhorse, is a good friend of mine."

"How do you know that it's really Johnny Boy?"

"We don't, but it's the only credible lead we have, so

we're going to pursue it," he responded. "Thanks to Arya, we should be able to verify if it's him or not."

"I'm going with you," Nova announced. "I want to be there when you take Johnny Boy down. He killed my witness."

"Nova…"

"Don't try to stop me, River. This is important to me."

After a moment, he nodded. "Clear it with Cohen. You will have to follow my lead."

"I can do that," she agreed. "Just let me go up and grab my bag. I keep one packed and ready to go."

As they headed out the door fifteen minutes later, Nova couldn't shake the dull sense of foreboding she felt.

"You just getting back?" River asked Kenny when he answered the door to his hotel room.

"Yep." He glanced over at Nova and grinned. "You tagging along?"

"I intend to do my part in taking down Johnny Boy," she responded. "It got personal when he killed Mateo."

Kenny nodded in understanding. "I feel you."

River quickly packed his travel bag, then set it on the floor across from the king-size bed. He was glad to have Nova along on this operation. She was calm under pressure and a great shot. He trusted her instincts.

But there was more.

For so long, River had believed he didn't deserve love, but Nova made him feel otherwise. Maybe once this was over… He stopped the thought from forming. He didn't like making too many plans when he was about to go on an operation like this. River wasn't worried about the outcome—he had confidence in his abilities and the team he was working with. But he knew all too well how things could go left in the blink of an eye.

He preferred to take it day by day.

Catching Johnny Boy would be a massive victory for the DEA and his career. River looked forward to the day he could look the drug trafficker in the face. There would be one less threat on the streets. He was smart enough to know that another would rise for each one they took down, but River would never stop fighting.

He glanced over at Nova. "Let's get out of here."

Downstairs in the lobby they waited for Kenny, who was still packing.

Fifteen minutes later, they were headed to the airport.

The drive was filled with a tense silence. River could feel the weight of their mission hanging in the air, suffocating any casual conversation they might have had. Nova stared out the window, seemingly lost in her own thoughts, while Kenny fiddled with the radio, searching for a distraction.

As they arrived at the airport, the atmosphere shifted. Energy crackled around them as travelers hurried by, oblivious to the dangerous game River and his team were about to play.

They made their way through security without incident, blending seamlessly into the bustling crowd.

River couldn't help but steal glances at Nova as they navigated through the maze of corridors. Something about her drew him in—the way she carried herself with unshakable determination, her unwavering loyalty to their cause. But it was more than that. Her presence offered him hope amid the darkness they were about to face.

They reached the gate just as their flight was boarding. River watched as the flight attendants checked tickets and passengers shuffled onto the plane. He could feel the anticipation building within him, knowing that this mission held the key to everything they had been fighting for.

River noticed a subtle shift in Nova's demeanor as they handed their tickets to the flight attendant. Her usually steely gaze softened, a flicker of vulnerability betraying her facade of strength. It was at that moment that he realized she was just as weighed down by the gravity of their task as he was.

The team settled into their seats.

River glanced out the window, catching a glimpse of his reflection in the glass. His face, worn with determination and sacrifice, revealed the toll of this impending fight on him. He wondered if there would ever be a time when he could be free and wouldn't have to bear the world's weight on his shoulders.

As the plane taxied down the runway, Nova turned to River, and their eyes locked briefly, a silent understanding passing between them.

They were in this together, no matter what lay ahead.

THE ENGINES DRONED ON, drowning out the noise of the doubts and fears that echoed within Nova's mind. The plane accelerated, and soon, they were airborne. The turbulence rattled the cabin, but she found solace in the chaos. It reminded her that even amid uncertainty and upheaval, she could still find her footing.

With each passing minute, their destination grew closer. They were heading into the heart of darkness, where victory awaited them or... Nova couldn't shake the feeling that this mission was different from all the others they had undertaken before.

She leaned closer to him, her voice barely audible over the whir of the engines. "River, this isn't going to be an easy fight. So far, Johnny Boy has been two steps ahead of us."

He turned to face her, his eyes filled with conviction.

"I know," River replied, his voice steady, although laced with concern. "But we've trained for this. And I've got you watching my back. I'm not worried."

Nova nodded, taking comfort in his unyielding confidence. River had a way of grounding her, reminding her that they were stronger together than apart. She squeezed his hand, their fingers intertwining in a silent promise to face whatever awaited them.

The once turbulent skies began to clear as the plane pierced through the dense clouds. The sun's golden rays spilled into the cabin, casting a warm glow that breathed life into Nova's troubled soul. It was as if the Lord offered His blessings for the mission ahead.

She was excited to meet the Shadow Wolves team, a group of elite operatives chosen for their unparalleled expertise in covert operations. Each member had their unique skills and backgrounds, but together they formed a formidable force, ready to face any challenge that came their way.

They landed two hours later.

A DEA agent based in Arizona picked them up and transported them to the base of their operations. The Shadow Wolves contingent and agents from the DEA and ATF awaited them.

"Are Redhorse and his team sure it's Johnny Boy?" Kenny asked in a low voice.

"As sure as any of us can be," River replied. "He was sighted in Sells, Arizona. Ray told me he could sneak into an area where cartel members were supposed to be on watch—instead, they were sleeping. He said he got close enough to get a pretty good look at the man. He believes that it's Johnny Boy. Not some look-alike."

"You're saying that he was basically in the cartel's camp,

and nobody saw him?" Nova questioned. "He'd have to be a *ghost*. Johnny Boy's too paranoid to sleep that deep."

"Ray's team nicknamed him Fade because of his uncanny ability to become a part of the scene without being detected," River said. "It means ghost or spirit, so you're right. I wouldn't be surprised if he slipped a sleeping aid in their coffee or something."

"Regardless, that's impressive," she responded.

"Wait until you see the Shadow Wolves in action," River said. "They can look at desert vegetation and tell how recently a twig has been broken, a blade of grass trampled by a human, or how many smugglers there are and which direction they were headed. I guess it's because they grew up comfortable with nature and know how to hear silent things and see the invisible in the desert."

"Wow," she murmured. "They have some serious tracking skills."

"Passed down from the elders, according to Ray," River said.

Nova looked up at him. "What about modern technology?"

"They have night-vision goggles, but it's been a while since I was on a task force with the Shadow Wolves," River answered. "What equipment they had back then didn't come close to the high-dollar toys the cartel can afford. But regardless of expensive technology, there still needs to be a person in the field. This is what the Shadow Wolves do well. They rely on traditional methods of tracking."

The room designated for the briefing was dimly lit, the air carrying a tangible air of anticipation. Nova fell into step behind River and Kenny as they made their way to a table situated in the middle, flanked by other law enforcement officials. The atmosphere buzzed with a mix of hushed conversations as everyone prepared for the critical briefing.

As Nova took her seat, she stole a glance at River. The presence of two additional US marshals entering the room brought a reassuring sense of unity. Cohen, her supervisor, had worked his magic with some last-minute negotiations to secure permission for Nova's involvement. Her father's collaboration with the local agency had played a crucial role several times in the past. Still, Nova's proven performance during the prior investigation with River had truly tipped the scales in her favor.

The dynamics of the room shifted subtly as the briefing commenced. Maps were spread across the whiteboard, detailing the intricate web of the upcoming operation. The plan unfolded like a chessboard, each move considered, calculated and executed with precision.

Nova's attention remained focused, her mind absorbing the details and contingencies. The room became a hive of activity, with agents discussing tactics, sharing intelligence and preparing for the challenges ahead. The collective expertise in the room allowed for a well-coordinated effort, a symphony of skills coming together for a common purpose.

One by one, the agents filed out of the room, each grabbing their tactical gear and checking their weapons before heading off to complete their final preparations.

Chapter Twenty-One

Nova stared out the window, taking in the rugged, mountainous landscape dotted with mesquite trees and cacti, as she, River and Kenny headed to the cartel's known location in the desert. The muted browns, yellows and greens were interrupted by occasional pops of vibrant red desert flowers. In the distance, a few humble buildings could be seen, signaling the location of tribal lands.

"I can see why the cartel would choose this terrain near the border," Kenny said. "It's wide-open land."

"It's desert," River responded. "Since Calderon's arrest, nearly half of the Mancuso drugs are now coming through Mexico and across the international boundary through the Tohono O'odham reservation."

They arrived at their destination twenty-five minutes later.

A muscular man approached and River conducted introductions between Nova, Kenny and Ray Redhorse.

Ray introduced his team. "We have another member," he said. "Ben Chee…he's out following a *sign*."

"What type of sign?" Nova asked.

"We use a technique called *cutting for sign*. Cutting is how we search for and evaluate a sign. This includes footprints, tire tracks, thread or clothing."

Nova listened with interest. "River said that you were able to sneak into a cartel camp once, and nobody saw you."

Nodding, Ray replied, "I'd been tracking them for a few hours. I waited until they made camp and fell asleep. Their spotter didn't even see me."

"You really are a ghost," Kenny said.

Nova nodded in agreement. She was in awe of Ray Red-horse and glad to have the Shadow Wolves accompanying them on this operation.

Ray chuckled. "I just try very hard not to get caught."

"The last time I was here, Ray made this incredible jack-rabbit stew," River said. "I'd never tasted any rabbit and wasn't interested in trying it, but he talked me into it. He cooked it over an open fire, which had a smoky flavor. It was *delicious*."

"I told River he'd starve if he didn't eat it," Ray responded with a chuckle.

"You made something else… It tasted like asparagus."

"Oh, the buds from a cholla cactus."

"The man is a ghost and can cook," Nova stated. "Now I'm really impressed."

"You haven't seen nothing yet," River responded.

RAY REDHORSE DROVE his truck slowly, with River, Nova and Kenny riding along. He kept his window open and carefully examined the ground as he drove.

"Anyone coming north had to travel this path," he explained.

Ray suddenly stopped and got out of the truck. He crouched down to study what seemed to be scrapes in the sand. "Looks like they tied carpet strips to their shoes. They're trying to hide their footprints."

"How long ago?" River asked.

"Most likely late yesterday." Ray pointed to a print. "See

that groove? A rat probably made it during the night. The traffickers could be far away by now."

Kenny sighed. "We missed them."

"This desert is huge," Ray said. "Traffickers don't rely on a specific route. They have a labyrinth of routes to utilize. The cartel uses spotters in the mountains to warn traffickers when to change their route."

"So, then we take out the *eyes*," River stated.

"The cartel will send a replacement," Ray responded. "We can take them down all day, but like ants…they'll just keep replacing them."

They all got back into the truck.

Ray drove down another path.

Fresh tire tracks shimmered in the sunlight, while older footprints overlapped with insect trails.

The three men got out of the truck a second time.

Ray fingered a burlap fiber snagged by the thorns on mesquite bushes. He held it to his nose, sniffing it. "This came from a bag filled with marijuana."

They scanned the area before climbing back into the vehicle. Ray drove around the mesquite bushes. "It's getting worse out here. Lately, we've had some problems with machine gun–wielding thieves lying in wait to steal drugs from the traffickers," he said. "And a couple of cartels fighting over ownership of certain routes."

"I see you have your friend with you," River said, referring to Ray's M4 assault rifle.

"I never leave home without it."

River glanced over at Nova. "How are you feeling about all this?"

"All I can think about is capturing Johnny Boy and his many minions. The Mancuso cartel robbed me of my father and a witness. I want to take down as many of them as possible."

"I understand," River responded. "They took out two DEA agents... One of them was like a brother to me."

The fire burning in her eyes mirrored his own. River knew they were kindred spirits fueled by a desire for retribution and justice. They both wanted nothing more than to dismantle the Mancuso cartel piece by piece.

"Nova," he said solemnly, "we will get Johnny Boy."

She nodded in agreement, her face etched with determination.

It was close to two o'clock when the joint task force spotted a ramshackle shack hidden amid the rocky terrain of the Arizona desert.

The air was thick with tension as they cautiously advanced, their weapons drawn and senses on high alert.

"All right, move in," barked Ray Redhorse, his voice terse with urgency.

With practiced precision, the team spread out, each member taking up a strategic position around the weathered structure.

River cautiously pushed it open.

Nova scanned the area, determined to see everything and everybody.

As they stepped inside, the pungent aroma of marijuana assaulted her senses, mingling with the musty scent of decay that permeated the air. Stacks of crates lined the walls while the floor beneath their feet was littered with discarded debris.

"Spread out and search the premises," ordered Ray, his eyes scanning the room for any signs of movement.

They heard a noise outside.

Two men tried to escape, from the sound of it, but had been apprehended.

"This is just the beginning," Ray declared, his voice resonating with determination.

As the sun began to dip below the horizon, their mission had been a success. They had taken down several scouting locations and captured those involved in trafficking.

But there was one crucial element missing.

Johnny Boy.

The team had been on the lookout for him, with no luck. However, their persistence paid off when they uncovered a massive stash of marijuana linked to the notorious Mancuso cartel. One of the men decided to talk after the agents seized 3,400 pounds of marijuana from the shack he was guarding.

"*Puedo ayudarle*...eh... I can help you," the scout repeated nervously, his eyes darting between each agent in the room. "I know where Johnny Boy is hiding."

Those words caught River's attention. "Where is he?"

The scout fidgeted nervously, knowing this was his only shot at survival. "*Acuerdo*...deal... I want deal."

River stepped closer, his gaze never wavering from the scout's face. "Speak quickly," he commanded. "Tell us everything you know about Johnny Boy and maybe we can offer you a chance at redemption."

The scout hesitated for a moment, his mind racing as he weighed his options. It was evident that fear wrestled with his desire to escape the clutches of the cartel. Finally, he gave in to his desperation and whispered, "Okay. I'll tell you..."

AFTER MIDNIGHT, River and a team of DEA agents and police officers were on the road to the small town of Pima,

Arizona. The scout had given up Johnny Boy's location—
a community in the desert outside of town. The Shadow
Wolves had remained behind at the arrest site to continue
monitoring movement in the desert.

"Wow…look at this place," said Nova when they arrived at their destination. "There's a grid-tied solar system,
a greenhouse…all miles away from the nearest neighbor."

River glanced around. This was the perfect place to hide
because it was so secluded. The three-story house was situated on eight or nine acres. There were orchards with apple,
peach, apricot, pomegranate and pear trees. Nearby was
a large fenced garden area and a metal shop warehouse.
He'd heard that Johnny Boy was vegan and preferred to
grow his own food.

His gaze returned to the home with the elaborate entry.
"It's a beauty. It'll be a shame to have to shoot up this house
if it comes to that."

They were a safe distance away from the property, waiting for the command to infiltrate.

"What do you think a place like this would cost?" Nova
asked.

"At least a couple million," River responded. "The floor
plan showed an Olympic-sized pool, a tennis court and a
basketball court. There's also a hair salon and barbershop
on-site. The guy has everything he needs."

"I'm surprised there's no guardhouse or men on roofs
with guns," Kenny interjected.

"My guess is that he's trying to blend in around here,"
River stated. "The guns are in the house and that building
over there…trust me."

He and other law enforcement fanned out around the
house and perimeter as they set out to capture and arrest
Johnny Boy. There was still the chance that he might have

fled already like a thief in the night, but River pushed the thought away.

We have to make sure we have every avenue covered.

River and the team crept to the porch steps of the house. Nova flanked him on the right.

He glanced over his shoulder, ensuring everyone was in position before gesturing to the officer to his right who was holding the ram waist-high.

River instructed the others to assume their positions, then gave the door a hard knock and yelled, "This is the DEA. *Open up.*"

No response.

River repeated the order sharply.

Again, nothing from inside.

He signaled to the officer standing behind him, then moved out of the way.

The officer drew the ram back, then swung it toward the door.

It didn't open.

He struck the door again, getting the same result.

River had enough experience to realize that the door was most likely barricaded on the inside. He also knew that they'd lost the element of surprise. Whoever was in the house had time in which to prepare a defense.

The officer repeatedly battered the door, forcing it to give way. It would open a few inches, but then immediately slam shut.

River swallowed his unease and stood directly in front of the entrance. He was able to steal a glance into the house for a split second, brief snapshots of figures moving about. He soon realized he was seeing a person—no, it was two people.

The officer slammed the ram once more.

River caught sight of a man with a shotgun aimed directly at the door.

"Gun," he yelled, ducking and pushing the officer out of the way just as a loud noise erupted from the interior of the house, leaving a hole in the door. Another round of bullets tore through the wood, forcing River to jump off the porch and into a cluster of bushes for cover. He glanced around, searching for Nova. She was safe, having taken cover behind a nearby tree.

He looked back at the house and caught a real glimpse of Johnny Boy—just as gunfire rang out all around him.

River felt a flash of raw pain and knew he'd been hit. Still, he drew his weapon and began firing into the house.

Out the corner of his eye, he saw one of the agents run to the left corner of the house. Another moved quickly to the right.

River touched his left side. His fingers were covered with warm blood. The wound throbbed as he felt blood spread across the front of his shirt.

I'm losing too much.

River tried to speak but couldn't think clearly. Everything started to spin, moving him toward a cloud of darkness.

In the distance, he heard someone saying, "We have an agent down…"

Nova rushed to his side. "We have to get you out of here. Hang on, River."

"Ken…" River managed.

"I'm right here," his partner uttered.

"No… Nova…" Every word took effort and all of River's strength.

"Don't try to talk," she responded. *"I'm here."*

Burning pain ripped through him.

"Where's the ambulance?" Kenny yelled. "*Call* them again."

River heard another round of gunfire nearby.

"Stay with him, Nova." Crouched low, his partner took off toward the side of the house.

A circle of darkness swirled around River, growing larger each minute until he couldn't see anything else. Waves of pain washed over him. He groaned with each wave.

Just before he was carried away on a sea of unconsciousness, River heard the loud shrill of sirens.

Chapter Twenty-Two

The journey from the perilous scene to hospital was a blur for Nova. As the medical team rushed River into surgery, she found herself directed to the waiting area, the weight of worry settling heavily on her shoulders.

The setting was different but it still reminded Nova of the night her father was killed by a cartel member.

"I can't lose him," she whispered, her words a silent prayer as she sat amid the sterile stillness of the hospital waiting room, every passing moment an agonizing eternity.

Time stretched until the door swung open, and a doctor entered.

His solemn expression carried the gravity of the situation, but his words brought a glimmer of hope. "Agent Randolph's surgery was a success. They were able to remove the bullets. Thankfully, no major areas suffered any real damage. He should be waking up anytime now. He'll be moved into his room after that."

Nova's sigh of relief was audible, the tension releasing from her like a held breath. "I'm relieved to hear it," she acknowledged, gratitude welling up as she realized that River had emerged from the brink of danger.

When Nova was finally allowed to see him, River lay sleeping, surrounded by the quiet hum of medical equipment.

She pulled a chair beside his bed and sat down, her gaze never leaving his face. The harsh fluorescent lights of the hospital room felt softer in these quiet moments, and Nova waited patiently for him to wake up, in a silent vigil by his side.

The steady beep of the heart monitor filled the room, a reassuring rhythm as she watched over River and hoped that he would awaken soon.

The room became a sanctuary of quiet anticipation. In this space, the echoes of worry were replaced by the promise of recovery and an unspoken bond forged between them.

RIVER OPENED HIS EYES, blinked several times, then opened them again. No doubt he was still feeling woozy from the anesthesia.

"Hey, you…" she said, relief and happiness flowing through her.

He turned his head. "Nova…"

"I'm here," she responded with a tiny smile. "You really scared me out there."

"I'll be fine," River said. Still feeling groggy, he closed his eyes. He opened them a few minutes later. "I'm sorry if I drifted off."

"You're good," Nova said. "Don't try to stay awake for me. I'm not going anywhere."

"Did we get Johnny Boy?"

Nova didn't want to be the one to tell River about the trafficker's escape. In the rush of the shoot-out, her only goal had been getting River the help he needed. But Kenny had called to fill her in that they hadn't made an arrest. "Kenny is on his way. He should be here soon."

When the nurse entered the room, Nova stood up. "I'm going to the cafeteria to get something to drink. I'll be right back."

"You don't have to leave," River said.

"I know. Don't worry. Not going far at all."

Nova walked out of the room just as Kenny stepped off the elevator.

"River just asked about Johnny Boy," she said, meeting him halfway. "I think you should be the one to tell him what happened."

He nodded, looking exhausted. "After all River's been through, I wish I could give him some much better news."

"The nurse is in the room with him right now," Nova stated.

"How are you holding up?" Kenny inquired.

"I'm relieved that he's still alive."

"Me, too." Kenny passed her, heading to River's room.

As she made her way to the elevator, Nova glanced up to see a tall man with long dreadlocks, a bouquet in hand, weaving through the corridors. His movements seemed purposeful, and a chill crept up Nova's spine.

Johnny Boy.

Instinct kicked in, and she followed him discreetly. He was so intent on his purpose that he never once looked in her direction. She was grateful her badge was hidden inside her pocket and that she'd removed the jacket that would've identified her as law enforcement.

Nova's eyes never left the bouquet, trying to see if it concealed potential danger.

The man moved with an eerie calmness, scanning room numbers with predatory intent. The dreadlocks swung with every measured step.

Nova's heart pounded as he drew closer to River's room.

When he produced what appeared to be a weapon from beneath the flowers, determination eclipsed her fear, and she stepped forward, calling out his name.

"Johnny Boy!"

He turned sharply, eyes narrowing as he saw Nova.

In that tense moment, the bouquet became a weapon. He threw it at her and fired a shot.

Nova's instincts propelled her into action; she lunged for cover. The bullet missed, leaving only the echo of gunfire in the hospital hallway.

Amid shocked screams, her eyes quickly bounced around to see if anyone had been shot.

Dropping the flowers to the ground without hesitation, Johnny Boy made a break for the stairwell, his hurried steps resonating in the hallway.

Nova, fueled by adrenaline and fierce determination, sprinted after him. The hospital staff, caught off guard by the sudden chaos, looked on in shock.

As Johnny Boy reached the second floor, Nova closed the gap.

Hospital security, alerted by the commotion, sprang into action. Responding to the urgency, they swiftly intervened, creating a human barricade at the bottom of the staircase.

Johnny Boy's escape route thwarted, Nova cornered him, her eyes locking on to his as she took aim.

"Drop the weapon!" she ordered.

His eyes darted around, taking in his situation.

The armed security closed in, acting in synchronized precision.

Smirking, Johnny Boy did as she instructed, then held up his hands in surrender.

Nova stood breathless, her gaze fixed on the man in custody. She was thrilled to see him in handcuffs.

When he was taken away, the hospital gradually returned to its usual hushed atmosphere, the threat extinguished, but the echoes of the confrontation lingered in the air.

"What happened?" Kenny asked when Nova returned to River's hospital room. "I heard gunshots."

"Johnny Boy was here," she announced. "I think he was planning to take out River."

"Where is he now?"

"In police custody. I called Special Agent Scott. I'm going to meet him at the precinct, but I wanted to check on River first."

"He's still groggy from the anesthesia and pain meds. I expect he'll probably be out until morning."

River opened his eyes just as Nova approached the hospital bed.

Nova could tell he was struggling to stay awake. "Stop fighting it. Go to sleep, River."

"No… I need to talk to Kenny."

"Here I am, partner."

She planted a kiss on his cheek. "I have to go."

He took her hand in his. "You will be back, though?"

"Yes. I'll get back as soon as I can."

"HEY, BUDDY," Kenny said when River woke up a second time. "You don't look so great."

"Just tell me that my getting shot was worth it," he responded. "Is Johnny Boy in jail?"

"He's in custody now." Kenny paused momentarily, then said, "He came to the hospital. Nova saw him and interrupted his plan."

"I thought I heard gunshots. Was I dreaming, or did that happen?" River asked.

"Naw, it was real. Right out in the hallway. Luckily, no one was hurt. Nova's on her way to the precinct now."

Nova's genuine concern, her quick actions in saving him, melted the final wall around River's heart. *Once I fully recover, she and I must sit down and talk.*

It was still a struggle for him to stay awake. "I need to close my eyes for a bit."

"You go right ahead," Kenny said. "I need to make some phone calls."

He fell back to sleep as he heard the door shut.

Chapter Twenty-Three

Nova wore a huge grin on her face as she exited the police precinct in the early morning hours.

The man captured at the hospital was not just another doppelgänger. The tattoo on his chest left no room for doubt—he was indeed John Boyd Raymond. His fingerprints had regrown, providing further evidence of his true identity. She silently thanked Arya for informing them about the tattoo and its significance.

Johnny Boy's arrogance was astonishing. He sat there smirking and laughing at them, unfazed that he was in custody or that he would be doing serious time for all the many crimes he'd committed.

He flat out refused to entertain any conversation, repeatedly saying, *"Lawyer."*

She'd left the interrogation room in frustration, wanting to get back to River.

She was looking forward to sharing the news that Johnny Boy had been arrested. He was Poppy's number one—his being in custody would shake up the cartel.

A sense of foreboding washed over her.

Maybe Johnny Boy didn't seem worried because he had a backup plan. There was a chance that River was still in danger.

Upon her return to the hospital, a palpable urgency to secure River's safety gripped Nova. Approaching the front desk with resolute determination, she flashed her badge and asserted, "I need Agent Randolph moved to another room immediately." Her tone conveyed a seriousness that couldn't be ignored.

The nurse behind the desk, eyes a mix of concern and fear, nodded in response. "Yes, ma'am."

Nova headed to his current room, passing a man with a cell phone to his ear, positioned a few feet away from the nurses' station. He was dressed in a pair of jeans and a Western-style shirt with cowboy boots. She homed in on him as she quickly approached River's room.

Both Kenny and River looked at her when she entered.

"What's wrong?" he asked.

"I requested to have you moved." Nova paused a heartbeat, then continued, "Johnny Boy's been arrested, but I'm not convinced that you're out of danger."

River nodded, looking less groggy than the last time she'd seen him. "See if it can be arranged for me to be flown to a hospital in Los Angeles."

A nurse came in to check his wounds and change his bandages, putting a temporary halt to their conversation.

"Has anyone been asking about me?" River asked.

"Not that I know of," the nurse replied. "Just so you know…we were instructed not to confirm that you're a patient here."

"That's great," Nova said. She showed her badge, then added, "I want the names of any nurses or doctors who will be caring for River. They are to be the *only* ones to come into his room."

"I'm working a double shift, so it will be me until seven a.m. tomorrow morning."

"I won't be leaving your side," Nova announced.

Kenny chuckled. "I had a feeling you'd say that. Can't say I'm surprised at all."

The rest of the morning passed without incident, and Kenny left the room to pick up some lunch for him and Nova.

She got up to go to the bathroom, leaving the door open just a tad in case River called for her.

Just after she washed her hands, Nova heard the door to the room open and close.

The nurse had checked on River at noon. The doctor wasn't expected to come back for another round until later in the evening.

Nova eased to the door and peeked into the room.

A lone figure moved stealthily toward the bed.

It was the man she'd seen earlier. Somehow, he'd been able to sneak into the room. He must have been watching the room and assumed River was alone after Kenny left.

Nova quickly assessed the situation. This man was bigger and stronger, but she wasn't about to leave River vulnerable to his attack. She fervently prayed that her boxing and self-defense lessons were about to pay off.

Using her foot, Nova eased the door open wider.

The man turned around, surprise evident on his face.

Nova saw the needle in his hand and wished she hadn't left her gun in her tote beside the bed.

He gave her a menacing look, then lunged at her.

Nova dodged and shoved the man off balance, forcing him to drop the syringe.

But it wasn't enough. He recovered, then sent a punch in her direction.

Agony tore through her as Nova took a hard hit to her right shoulder.

She cocked back her uninjured arm and threw a jab as hard as she could. It connected with his jaw. Kicking out, Nova connected her foot into the man's knee, bringing him down.

Nova squeezed her eyes closed as she tried to breathe through the pain ripping from her shoulder and down her arm. The tendons in her left hand were on fire, but Nova wasn't about to let up. She punched the attacker's face again, then a third time.

In the distance, she heard River talking, but she couldn't understand what he was saying.

She had no sense of time or place as she put all her energy into knocking the man unconscious. Nova had no awareness of when Kenny rushed in with hospital security.

Someone—she didn't know who—pulled her off the man.

The room was soon filled with hospital staff. Some were checking on River while others placed the man on a gurney, handcuffed him and pushed him out of the room.

"Nova," River called out. "You okay?"

Kenny assisted her over to the chair. "You should let them look at your shoulder."

"I'm good," she said. "He landed a solid punch. I'll be sore for a few days but that's about it." Her gaze was on River. She evaluated him, making sure he was okay. Satisfied that River was safe, Nova lowered her eyes, searching the floor. "Kenny, over there... He came in here with a syringe."

Kenny slipped on a pair of gloves from a nearby counter before picking it up. "I'll send this to our lab."

Nova's eyes traveled back to where River lay in bed. "You sure you're okay?" he asked again.

She nodded. "I'm good."

But the truth was that she was anything but okay. Nova could have very easily taken that man's life to save River. But this time it had nothing to do with her sense of duty as a law enforcement officer. It was different because she was protecting the man she loved.

RIVER WAS MOVED into a new room with twenty-four-hour security. The doctor felt he was too weak to be moved to a hospital in California.

Nova hardly left his side for the next two days. River was concerned that she wasn't getting enough rest.

"You should go with Bonnie to the hotel," he told her. His sister had arrived this morning. He was glad that she and Nova were getting along so well.

"I'm good. Don't you start worrying about me," Nova assured him. "Focus on getting better so we can get you home."

She sank into the visitor chair. "I can tell you're feeling much better. You're starting to get bossy."

He tried to laugh but it hurt.

They talked for a little while until River noticed she could barely keep her eyes open. Ten minutes later, she was sound asleep.

River eased out of bed and held on to the portable IV stand for support. He crossed the short distance to the bathroom.

His business done, he made his way back to bed, sagging with relief when he eased his body under the covers.

Bonnie had tried to convince him to use the portable urinal for another day or so, but his pride just wouldn't let him. He'd argued that he needed to move around to regain his strength. Right now, he was out of breath and in extreme pain. The medication helped to take the edge off, but the sheer effort it took for him to get out of bed and go to the bathroom—it almost wasn't worth it.

River felt bad that he hadn't helped Nova fend off the attacker who'd come into his room, but she'd managed well. He could only press the call button and hope someone would arrive in time. He'd tried to pull the chair closer to the bed in hopes of getting to the gun he knew was inside the tote.

He knew that Nova had had the same goal—she'd wanted to retrieve her weapon but couldn't. Still, she'd managed to subdue the man.

River had done a silent assessment of his own, making sure she wasn't seriously hurt. He caught her wincing every now and then, but Nova had refused to be examined. She kept telling the nurse and the doctor that she was fine. He felt that was because she didn't want to leave his side—she was in what he called *guard* mode.

Later that evening, River signaled to his sister and Kenny to give him a moment alone with Nova.

"Kenny, we haven't had a chance to talk," Bonnie said. "Why don't you take me to dinner? I don't mean to the cafeteria either."

"I'd love that, actually," he responded with a grin.

"Did I miss something?" Nova asked when she and River were alone.

"Kenny met my sister a few years ago," he responded. "As far as I know, it's not been anything outside of harmless flirting here and there."

"Oh, okay."

"Nova…you saved my life. Thank you."

"I was just doing my job." She shook her head. "No, that's not true. River, all I saw was that the man I loved more than life itself was in danger. He was going to kill you and I had to stop him."

He couldn't help but feel a swell of pride and love for her

in that moment. She saw him as the man she loved with all her heart. And in that instant, as his life hung in the balance, she risked everything to protect him. He couldn't believe how lucky he was to have someone like her by his side, willing to sacrifice herself for his safety.

"I wondered what was going on in your mind. I'd never seen you filled with such rage. Kenny had to pick you up to keep you from punching the man to death. He deserved it, as far as I'm concerned."

"I'd do it again," Nova said smoothly.

He gestured for her to sit on the bed beside him.

"You're supposed to be resting."

"What's the plan? I know you're working on something in that brain of yours."

"As soon as you're strong enough to fly, I'm taking you to Los Angeles to continue your recovery."

River nodded in approval. "Sounds good to me."

"I meant to check to see if he had any ID on him."

"Kenny most likely took care of all that," River said. "I'm just glad nobody else got hurt." He paused a moment, then added, "I wish you'd let someone check out your shoulder. I know it's bothering you."

Nova eyed him. "I'm good. My shoulder is a bit sore and my hand's swollen but not broken. That's it."

"You'd tell me the truth, wouldn't you?"

"Yeah."

River took her left hand in his. "I heard what you said, Nova. I would prefer to have that discussion when I'm not under the influence of pain meds."

She smiled. "I can wait."

FIFTEEN DAYS LATER, River was out of the hospital and home. Nova had finally convinced him to take a nap. He'd been up most of the morning after a follow-up visit to the doctor. Her gaze traveled her surroundings. The dove-gray walls and deep navy-colored drapes provided a rich backdrop while soft music floated throughout the house. River had a fantastic view of palm trees, the beach and the Pacific Ocean.

He had contemporary furnishings. The dining area was large enough for a table of six and overflowed in the open great room. She especially loved the teal-and-silver color scheme of the kitchen.

"Did you decorate this place by yourself?" Nova asked when he woke up an hour later.

He nodded. "Yeah, I did."

"You have a really nice home."

"Thanks. When are you going to start looking for a place out here?"

"I don't know," Nova responded. "Right now, I just want to make sure your recovery goes well. I must confess that I have zero nursing skills, but I'll make sure your bandages and the area around the wound are kept clean and dry. The doctor says you're healing nicely."

He smiled. "You'd probably do a better job than I would."

Nova rearranged his pillows so River could sit propped up.

"Thanks," he said.

"Your doctor said you could use an ice pack on the bandage to help with swelling. Do you have one?"

Nodding, River replied, "There's one in the freezer."

She picked up her iPad. "Let me check my notes. I want to make sure I'm not missing anything."

"Nova, you can relax." River chuckled. "You're doing great."

She released a short sigh. "Are you in any pain?"

He shook his head no. "I'm fine."

River patted the empty space beside him. "Sit down and talk to me."

"You should get some rest," Nova stated.

"I will."

"When you were shot…it reminded me of the night I lost my father." Her eyes teared up. "I'd never been so scared."

River took her hand in his own. "When I thought I was dying, all I could think of that night was you and how much I wanted to see that beautiful smile of yours. I was filled with so many regrets. I promised I'd make some changes if I was given the chance."

"Like what?" Nova asked.

"I've spent most of my life afraid to give my love to anyone for fear of rejection. Then I met you."

"And I broke your heart."

"That's all in the past," River said. "Back then, it might not have worked out. I think we were both trying to sort out our individual issues. Now we're older and wiser…"

"I'd like to think so," Nova responded.

"Back then, I thought we had something. Then I realized that you weren't ready for a relationship. I do believe that you cared for me, but I also believe that you aren't ready to make a commitment."

"I panicked, River, but that's all changed now," Nova said. "I want to be with you. Can't you see that?" She kissed him. "What we have is worth fighting for," she whispered.

His voice cracked with emotion as he asked her, "But can you handle the tough times that come with love? Will you stay and fight when things get difficult?"

She tightened her grip on his hand and looked into his eyes. "I already proved it when I risked my life to save yours," she said firmly.

He needed to hear it from her own lips that she was willing to stay and fight for their love.

Nova met his gaze. "You know that I love you. I'm not afraid anymore. River, I'm so sorry for the pain I caused. I would rather cut off my own hand before I ever hurt you again."

When he didn't respond, she said, "River, I'm the only woman for you."

"That you are," he confirmed. "I've never met anyone who makes me feel what you do. There was a time when I wanted to forget you, but I couldn't. My heart wouldn't let me. *You* wouldn't let me."

"Then I need to hear *you* say that you're ready to give me a second chance."

"I'm ready to take another chance at love..." River said. "With you."

Epilogue

Six months had passed since Nova decided to relocate to Los Angeles, leaving Charlotte behind and embracing a new chapter in her career with Rylee's task force, whose sole focus was targeting high-level drug cartel organizations such as the Mancuso cartel. She felt a sense of freedom that she never had with the Marshals.

She found herself thriving in the fast-paced environment, fueled by the adrenaline of her work and the camaraderie of her fellow agents.

Amid the chaos of their demanding jobs, Nova found solace in the arms of River. Their relationship had blossomed in the months since her arrival, growing stronger with each passing day as they navigated the highs and lows of their shared journey. Together, they forged a bond built on trust, respect and a deep-seated love that defied the odds.

The sound of Kaleb's voice cut into her musings.

"We received intel that Poppy has a new number one," Kaleb stated. "They're being very secretive about this one."

"Well, it's only a matter of time before we find out who he is," Rylee responded confidently.

"Nova, I know that this is never going to bring your father back, but it might help," Kaleb said after the meeting ended.

"It won't, but I'd still like to make as many of the Mancuso cartel members pay for what they've done," she responded.

"I'm alive because of Easton," Rylee stated. "If I have anything to say about it, we'll keep chipping away at Poppy's organization until we get to her."

Grinning, Nova shot back, "I'm here for it all."

"That's it for now. Operation Reckoning is live…"

* * * * *

HARLEQUIN
Reader Service

Enjoyed your book?

Try the perfect subscription for Romance readers and get more great books like this delivered right to your door.

See why over 10+ million readers have tried Harlequin Reader Service.

Start with a Free Welcome Collection with free books and a gift—valued over $20.

Choose any series in print or ebook. See website for details and order today:

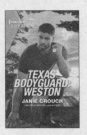

TryReaderService.com/subscriptions